RED PALACE

THE WHITE HART TRILOGY
BOOK TWO

SARAH DALTON

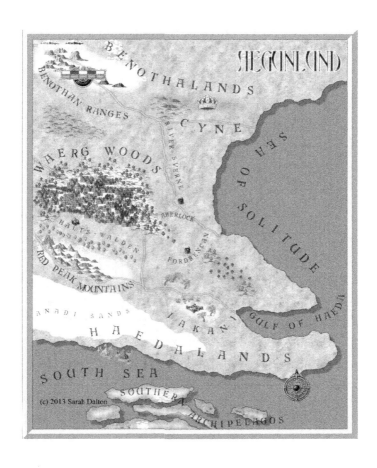

CHAPTER ONE

THE SLEEPING PALACE

Silence in the Red Palace is as unnatural and strange as snow on the Anadi sands. As I stalk the gloomy palace basement, unease grips me by the throat. Fear shakes energy into my muscles, turning me into a quivering mess. I circle the sleeping bodies over and over as though if I keep moving around them, they will wake up and all this will be some sort of mistake.

But it is no mistake. The flip of my stomach tells me that whatever has gone wrong, it is in part my own doing. I triggered some sort of curse when my blood hit the Soil of the Ancients, and now the court of Cyne lay in slumber at my feet—draped over the cold flag stones like abandoned dolls.

As the magic spreads, a silky dust spreads over the scene. My nostrils become clogged with it and my eyelids chalky. The air is thick with rot. The stench hits the back of my throat and I gag. Before my eyes, the castle becomes as still as winter; cobwebbed, grey, and decaying. The lights no longer flicker. Life has gone.

When the shock subsides, I drop to my knees next to Cas. I have to wipe the dirt away from his face before I lower my ear to his mouth. My shoulders slump with relief when his breath tickles the hairs by my temples. He's alive. But no matter how vigorously I shake him, he doesn't wake. There's some sort of foul play at work here. Ever since I helped Ellen reignite the craft with my blood, some sort of magic has plunged the Red Palace into slumber. With the scattering dust it is as though I have been trapped here a decade, yet it has been mere moments.

I pick my way around the fallen bodies, checking pulses and breath. None of them will wake, not Ellen or the king, or Beardsley or the queen… they lay on the flagstones, skin and clothes coated in grime, like neglected ornaments.

"I need help," I say to no one.

Tripping over my feet, I dash down the corridor, past the great furnaces, up the steps and into the ballroom. Minutes ago this room had been filled with dancing merrymakers. The tables had been piled high with platters of delicious fruits. Now, I lift a hand to my nose against the stench. Putrefied food disintegrates onto the silver platters. Serving girls and butlers are slumped over tables, their limbs dangling towards the castle floor. No one moves.

My footsteps echo; bouncing from the high ceilings and reverberating from the walls. My heartbeat quickens as I realise how alone I am. With my fists gripping the sides of my skirt, I rush over to a window. Outside, the city of Cyne seems quiet and still. Leaning forward over the stone wall so that it squashes my chest, I wave my arms frantically, and call to those below me.

"Hello!"

No movement at all.

"Help!"

I realise then that the city is deserted. There isn't a single soul making their way through the markets and establishments. With a sinking feeling, I think of Anta in the stables alone. Is he frozen in slumber like the others? It panics me, and I try to lean further over the sill until my head is out of the palace completely, but it's like my forehead hits a barrier. Some sort of magical force field prevents me from putting even a finger outside the castle. It's as though there is an invisible barrier wrapped around the building. I gasp. What if I am trapped?

I lean back and grip the stone sill with my fingers, mustering every ion of strength. Then, I yell, loud as I can, hardly even forming the word "help", merely screaming, until I feel the tendons strain from my neck. My throat is scrubbed raw by the time I stop. It takes a few seconds to recover, and during that time my eyes scan the city below, praying to all the Gods I know that someone, somewhere, heard me.

Nothing.

Breath escapes my lungs in a rush. I can't be trapped in the castle. I can't be stuck in here, the only conscious soul, with lives to save. What will I do? What *can* I do?

"No, no, no," I mumble, backing away from the window.

I turn and sprint towards the castle hallway, tripping on the hem of my dress and stumbling over spilled goblets. I pass slumped guards on my way. Their swords lay dormant at their sides. With a second thought I stop running and reach down to unbuckle a guard's belt, releasing the sword and the scabbard. There aren't enough belt holes to fit it against my narrow hips, so I have to knot the belt loop through the buckle. The sword hangs low and heavy on my body, but at least I have a way to protect myself.

I return to my task.

I know that on this side of the castle is a small doorway that leads to the courtyard before the great wall into Cyne. Perhaps I can at least make my way into the courtyard. What I can do then, I don't know, but I have to try.

The wooden door looms ahead and I collide with it, too anxious to slow myself to a stop. I count down from ten before throwing all of my weight against the bar across the door, my forearms straining. Not a groan or a shove will shift it. The thing is stuck.

When I weaken from the effort I take a step back, wiping away the sweat from my forehead. There's only one thing I can try now. I have to call upon the craft.

I take a deep breath to calm my fluttering heart. The image of Cas laid out on the floor tightens my chest in panic, but I push that thought away and concentrate on the matter at hand. If this is a magical curse, perhaps it can be broken by my magic. I've used the craft before, I've even used it to defend myself, but there are times when it is difficult to control. I've learned the hard way that emotions can throw me off course, even hurt the people around me. I've known it to blast through me like an uncontrollable force of destruction. Then there are times when it doesn't work at all. But it is all I have: my weapon, my gift, my one true power.

Summoning the craft takes all of my focus. The air shifts around me. My hair lifts. I call upon air to help me break through the door, to rip the wood from its hinges and tear it through the castle courtyard. A hurricane storms through the hallway, knocking tapestries and suits of armour to the stone floor. I am immune, and I stand with my arms stretched out wide, waiting for the door to break.

It holds steady.

In the Borgan camp, I lost control of my powers. The tornado had grown so powerful that it took all of my concentration to keep it under control. I'd destroyed huts and belongings that day. It is something I will never stop being ashamed of. But all of that means that I should at least be able to knock the wooden barrier from the door.

I frown. Perhaps I didn't try hard enough.

The second attempt is a tornado that whips up the carpet and even shatters a large mirror on its journey down the hallway. Still the door remains locked. And after that, I try to summon nature. Birds and butterflies appear at the windows from my request, but they can't come in, and they can't move the door. I try to talk to them, but somehow I get the feeling they can't hear me anyway.

The hopeful swell in my chest dissipates after an attempt to make the earth shift below the door. Instead, I cause a little more than a slight rupture between the stones. But, there is dirt! Without a second thought I drop to the floor and begin digging. Maybe I can tunnel my way out of the castle to find help. I start with my hands, but the dirt is solid. I try the sword, seeing if I can pierce the ground at all. The magic prevents me from even breaking into it. My hopes of tunnelling are quashed.

I back away and half collapse against the wall. If I can't open the door to the castle, chances are I can't escape from any part of it, not from the bell tower, or any of the windows, or through the dungeon. The magic is too strong.

Someone set this up. They cursed the palace, knowing what would happen. And they used *my* magic to do it.

But who? And how?

I have only known of two individuals to channel my magic, the first being Ellen, and the second, Allerton, the leader of the Borgans. Both of them used an amber coloured amulet to pull the craft from me. But what would a Borgan gain from this? Who stands to gain from sending the palace into a slumber? I shake my head and pull myself onto my feet. My muscles ache from summoning pointless powers.

It's a shaky walk back into the basement, and on the way I pass the silent engines of the great palace. It's strange not to see the dirtied men shovelling coal into the great fires, or the moving pistons sending steam into the air, keeping the palace alive. Without the engines, the special lights no longer blink, and the kitchen cookers are cold. I run a finger along the metal tubes, when I remove it, black coal dust stains my skin. The silence is unbearable, and after many attempts to open the castle door, I feel alone and dejected on the long walk down the castle tunnel. It takes a touch from the locket hidden under my dress to inspire me with the confidence to go on. What would father say if I gave up now?

Perhaps if I drop my blood back onto the sacred earth it will break the curse. It sounds too simple, but I have to try. I pull the ceremonial dagger from Ellen's hand—the one she pretended to use after I gave her my blood so it would look like she is the craft-born—and run it along my palm, wincing at the pain.

"Please." I squeeze my hand over the bowl of soil and think of my powers. I imagine each element filling me up until I'm whole. The earth, air, wind and fire fuel me, fuel my gift. Precious drops of blood spill onto the soil, but nothing happens. Not even a twinge. During the ritual I'd experienced an overload of sensations, hearing the waves of the sea, smelling the dewy grass of nature, and feeling the heat of fire on my cheek. I'd felt them deep within me. This time the magic is dead.

After losing enough blood to make me woozy, I sit down on the floor next to Cas, tearing a strip of material from my dress to bandage the wound on my hand. I didn't survive the Waerg Woods to be thwarted by a curse. There has to be some way around this.

I sigh. And then there is Anta, out there in the castle stables. I have no way of getting to him if I cannot leave the palace. I can only hope that he is safe, and that when I lift the curse I will be able to go to him again.

Cas looks so peaceful. I can't help it. I reach out to his face and my fingers brush his hair. He will never love me, but we will always have that one journey together. I stroke his face — wondering how I can make him wake up — when a voice pops into my head. A voice I recognise, and one that makes the blood drain from my face.

I am here when you run from me,
You cannot touch me, but I make you cold.
I am there in the faint of heart,
But rarely with the daring, and bold.

Who am I?

I gasp as a sudden sensation of falling, no, being sucked downwards, pulls me from consciousness. I reach out and claw the air in front of me, as though trying to find purchase; gripping onto nothing. The room goes black.

The next moment there is an explosion of colour. The air is scented lavender and powdery, like the expensive talc Ellen and the queen use. Skirts twirl and the boots of men chase them. Women's laughter ripples over the sound of a string orchestra as it plays a slow, melodic tune. When I look up, a glittering chandelier sparkles as bright as the stars on a clear night.

My breaths seem shallower, and when I try to fill my lungs, it's as though there is a fist gripping my chest. I examine myself, confused by this restriction, to find a tight corset around my waist. I'm encased in a gown of deep blue. It's soft to the touch and balloons out into a full skirt which trails the floor. The sleeves float as I move my arms, but a chill around my neck reveals that the neckline is low. I would never wear this dress in a million years, and yet here I stand, in the middle of a ballroom, surrounded by dancers who glide like they are on ice. Why?

It's certainly a fancy dance. The kind where waiters walk with one hand tucked behind their upright backs, holding out silver trays filled with tiny portions of delicious treats. I steal one, moving away before someone fathoms that I shouldn't be here.

How did I get here? As I lap the room, strange images flash before my eyes, sights that turn my stomach—like maggoty bread and disintegrating apples. In a flash those images disappear, replaced with piles of sweet pastries and tiny cakes stacked into towers.

No one seems to notice me. Party-goers stand around in gaggles, sipping from their champagne flutes and laughing loudly. The men wear britches with high-waists and loose tunics. The women are encased in dresses with bone-crunchingly tight corsets and large round skirts. All the guests wear masks. I find mine tucked into the pocket of my dress, so I put it on. Handy clips keep it in place.

I back away from the tables and slip into the shadows by a long drape. It's here that the ballroom tapers into an entrance with a strange little man holding a scroll. A tall, silver, powdered wig sits atop his head, curled into tight ringlets that are piled high like stacked scrolls. His face has been covered in white make-up and there is a little red heart-shaped mouth drawn over his lips. A tiny black heart is sketched on his cheek.

"Psst."

I spin on my heels. I'm unused to the extra height, causing me to lose my balance and almost topple over. Behind me, the drape twitches. I narrow my eyes and take a step forward. Did the curtain just... speak?

"Wh-what?"

"Psst," it says again.

I shuffle towards the drapes, beginning to worry about my sanity.

"Um, is someone there?" I whisper.

The curtain twitches and a hand appears from behind the drapes. A tiny hand. After the hand comes a tiny face, with bright silver eyes. They brim with tears.

"Can you see him?" the boy says. He must be around seven years old.

"Who?" I ask.

"My brother." The small fingers grip hold of the drapes so tightly that his knuckles pale. "He was chasing me with a whip." The boy shudders.

"Well, that's horrible. Did you whip him back?" I say.

The boy shakes his head. "He's bigger than me. Even though I'm a year and a half older. I *hate* my brother. He's a brute."

"You should fight back you know, then he won't hurt you anymore."

"If I fight back, Father locks me in the cupboard and won't let me have supper. He says the future king shouldn't be beaten by someone younger than me. He says I'm a mummy's boy and I need to learn."

"Your father is the king?" I ask.

The boy nods sadly. "Yes." He pulls the drape back a little further. "Can I tell you a secret?"

"Of course."

"You promise not to tell anyone?"

I draw across my heart with my fingers. "Cross my heart."

"I don't like my father or my brother, and I don't want to be king. But, I know I have to be king or Lyndon will rule the realm. That wouldn't be good."

"I'm sure you'll be a very good king one day," I say. "You already sound much nicer than your brother and your father."

"What's your name?" the boy asks.

"Mae," I reply.

"Father says I shouldn't talk to commoners, but Mother says I should try to learn everyone's names. I like your name."

"Your mother sounds very wise," I muse. I turn away and scan the crowd, suddenly curious that the king and queen are in this room. When I turn back to the little boy, he's gone. "Strange," I whisper.

I let the curtain fall back and step away. My footsteps echo against the hard wood floors.

It's only then that I realise the music has stopped. The room has emptied. The ballroom is gone. All that's left is an eerie sound that I know I've heard somewhere before: *click-ick-ick-click...*

I trip over on my silly high-heeled shoes and take a tumble on the floor. As I fall it's like my insides are being pulled down, sucked down faster and faster...

CHAPTER TWO

THE RETURN OF THE BORGAN

I yank my hand back from Cas's face and clutch my chest. What just happened? I wipe a slick of sweat from my forehead and try to calm my breathing. What did I see? What did I *feel*? What did I hear?

It takes me a moment to recognise the basement of the palace and the sleeping people spread along the floor. The familiar musty smell brings me back to my senses; it brings with it the panicked, trapped feeling of being stuck in the castle.

"Cas, what are you showing me?" I whisper. I let my fingers move closer to him, to brush his skin. I wonder if touching him again will plunge me into his world, but this time nothing happens. Not even when I place my palm on his forehead. It seems I am not in control of whatever vision is being shown to me. I decide to move along to another sleeping body and see if the same thing happens. After all, Cas isn't the only person who needs help. I can't let myself be sucked into a world I never want to leave. I have to wake everyone in the castle, not just those I love.

Then I remember, and my stomach sinks. I had heard a voice before the vision. A voice I have heard only once before, and the memory of that voice, plus what it represents, is enough to nauseate me.

The Nix.

I close my eyes, trying to block away thoughts of the Waerg Woods: my legs encased in its freezing serum, the events it showed me, my own fears, the way I woke with the sharp stone in my hand, ready to hurt myself...

It had spoken to me in my mind as it always does. And in the vision I had heard the sound of it moving, the clicking of the great shells along its back. A shudder runs down my spine as I think of its large, insect-like body, and the many crawling legs, and the circular shaped mouth filled with a spiral of teeth. If it is here in the palace... I shake my head. I cannot lose hope. I must focus on the words it spoke to me. It was some sort of riddle:

I am here when you run from me,
You cannot touch me, but I make you cold.
I am there in the faint of heart,
But rarely with the daring, and bold.

Who am I?

Back home in Halts-Walden, the only people who ever told riddles were the travelling bards and mummers. But they rarely came to our village because of our proximity to the Waerg Woods. I've only heard a few riddles in my life and am not particularly good at solving them. I ruminate on the lines, embedding them in my memory, whispering them into the quiet castle, all the time with my skin tingling at the thought of the Nix being out there somewhere, watching, waiting. What does it want from me?

I am here when you run from me

That sounds like the Nix itself.

I am there in the faint of heart

I stand up and walk around the basement, looking at the sleeping people. The queen, her head turned to one side, Lyndon with his mouth set in a firm line, the king, oddly vulnerable with his eyes shut, and Beardsley, blending into the white cobwebs. When I come to Ellen, a spider runs across her full lips and it makes me shudder. I shoo it away with the toe of my boot. As I gaze at her open face, the voice comes again, with the same words:

I am here when you run from me,
You cannot touch me, but I make you cold.
I am there in the faint of heart,
But rarely with the daring, and bold.

Who am I?

This time I'm ready for it. The sucking pulls me down, but I remain in control of my consciousness. In a flash I'm back in Halts-Walden. The bright sun sets my skin tingling. I sit on the knoll of a riverbank overlooking the mill, my muscles relaxed, my thoughts calm. The grass is warm beneath my fingertips, and there's a sense of contentment that I'm not used to. The air smells sweet, with traces of honeysuckle from the nearby garden.

I'm humming to myself and fiddling with my long hair—a gorgeous raven colour. My voice is not my own, it is prettier, and melodic in a way I could only dream of sounding. My hands are not my own. They are creamy in complexion and more delicate. The callouses I have acquired from climbing trees are now gone.

But this time I am more aware of what is happening around me. I understand that this is some sort of vision. I know I am in Ellen's body and that this is in her mind. It's almost as though I am accessing her memories and her experiences.

A blonde girl walks towards me and my heart soars.

"Alice!"

It's not me who focusses on her golden hair or the way her dress hugs her narrow waist, it's the body I'm visiting.

"Ellen!" She grins and breaks into a run. "Look! I have daisies to put in your hair."

Ellen's body flushes with joy, and yet I *feel* it as though it is my own. I feel the blood rush to her cheeks and her chest constrict with worry.

"Will you braid my hair?" she asks. There is a tremor of vulnerability in her voice. She is

24

nervous, something I never imagined of Ellen. Especially not back in Halts-Walden.

"Of course, sweet girl." Alice's skirt rustles as she places herself next to Ellen — and me — on the grass and she gathers my — Ellen's — hair in her hands. "I wish I had hair as soft as yours."

"Alice, your hair shines like the sun. Why in all of Aegunlund would you want hair like mine?" Ellen's heart is pounding against her ribs and her cheeks remain flushed with blood.

It's strange that she feels this way in the mere presence of her friend. I remember Ellen always being in Alice's company. They would walk around the village holding hands, shoving their little noses in the air like they owned it all. The way she feels now is exactly like the strange way my body reacts around Cas. I never know what words or innocent touches will make my cheeks burn with embarrassment.

Alice's fingers braid Ellen's hair with deft precision. Every now and then she pauses to show Ellen her handiwork, pulling the braid around to reveal tiny daisies woven like jewels through the strands of black.

"Alice?" Ellen asks. Here I sense the trepidation in her voice and the slight shake emerging in her hands. "Do you think we could do it again?"

Alice pauses for a moment. She tugs on the plait once, then wraps it around Ellen's head, holding it in place with pins that dig against her skull. Ellen winces.

"I don't think we should." Alice speaks in a hushed tone, rough and fast.

"Of course," Ellen says. "You're right. Have you... have you wanted to since the last time?"

"No," Alice snaps. "Because it is forbidden."

Ellen bows her head, staring at the grass below. There's a sickness in her churning stomach that is at odds with the girl I used to know. She wraps her arms around her body and hugs herself. One word pops into her mind but she doesn't say it aloud. *Shame.*

Alice moves to face Ellen. Her lips are puckered and her eyelids half closed as though in contemplation of her actions. She lets out a sigh and tucks an errant strand of hair behind Ellen's ear.

"I have wanted to. Very much," Alice says. "But it is wrong."

"I know," Ellen replies. Tears burn behind her eyelids and she blinks rapidly to keep them at bay. "I'm sorry I mentioned it."

Alice turns her head and looks around

them. "Well, we are alone."

Ellen's heart soars again. Blood thuds in her ears. "Yes, we are." When she speaks, her voice is breathy.

The grassy knoll, the soft swing of the mill, the lapping of the river, the birds in the trees, they all melt away. There is only Alice. Her hair smells like rosemary and lemons. Ellen's fingers rise to her cheek, touching the smooth skin and tracing a line to her ear. Both Alice and Ellen lean into each other, and when their lips touch, Ellen's heart flutters.

She tastes like honey and her mouth is warm. Inside Ellen's body, I'm aware of how bawdy songs from the tavern described this act as against the Gods, an insult to Celine, yet I'm also aware of how it feels to Ellen. It seems natural to her, like breathing. How can that be? It goes against how we are brought up.

In that instant I question everything I'm taught, because none of those who preach could possibly understand the true meaning of the world and of the universe. They don't even know what the Gods want or believe. I am aware of my gift in this moment. There is nothing more powerful and true than the nature in my powers, and the love Ellen feels stirs the powers within. That is my truth now.

In the next instant I'm ripped away.

Ellen's panic becomes my panic. Never before have I felt so trapped.

"Get off her!" the miller booms.

"Daddy," Ellen says. Tears swell as her stomach twists with fear.

A rough hand yanks her up, grasping the collar of her dress, and Ellen can only stare down at Alice who sits with her hand over her mouth, looking up with wet eyes.

"Daddy, please."

Another yank tears Ellen away from her love. Ellen's shoes drag across the grass as she's pulled away. Hot water falls down her cheeks and she struggles against the large man.

"You make me sick, you little whore," he growls.

Ellen cries out as she's thrown into the small cottage the Millers call home, a place I had often been jealous of. I will never be jealous of Ellen again.

"Husband, what is happening?" Ellen's mother—an attractive and slightly plump woman in an apron—rushes to her daughter's aid, helping her up and away from the man.

"I caught her at it with a farmer's daughter. That *Alice*." He says her name in a hiss.

"Oh, Ellen," says the Miller's wife. "We

talked about this—"

"You knew!" he booms. "You're in on it together? Two whores trying to trick an old man like me!"

His face turns red and his fists clench by his side. The Miller is a hefty man, but not someone I had ever considered violent. If anything, Father and I had often made fun of him being hen-pecked by his wife and daughter. As one of the wealthiest in the town, he often flashes his coin in the tavern or comes back from Fordrencan with new cloth for dresses. We had always assumed the women in his life were the cause of his spending. Now I know differently. Perhaps those gifts were bought out of guilt for violent outbursts.

The Miller strikes his wife across the face and Ellen catches her as she falls backwards. Ellen screams as the Miller approaches her, grabbing her by the throat and pulling her to her feet. Her pain is mine. Her panic is mine, too, and my throat burns from his tight grip.

I think of those absences from school. It wasn't because Ellen thought she was better than the rest of us. It's because she had bruises that needed to fade.

"You're an abomination," he says. "You make me sick."

Ellen claws at his fingers, but the Miller slaps her around the face with the back of his hand. I feel the smart as though I had been hit myself. My cheek stings from the blow.

"I had high hopes for you. You were supposed to marry the prince and become a queen." He yanks an amulet from inside her bodice. It's almost identical to the one I saw Allerton wielding in the Borgan camp. It harnesses my own magic. "I got you this to make it happen." He tightens the chain around her neck until Ellen is gasping for breath. "But you disrespect me with your whorish dresses and by whoring yourself out in the most perverted of ways."

The panic gurgles in Ellen's throat. Rough gulps of air become stuck in her windpipe while her lungs burn with asphyxiation.

He throws her back and she staggers towards a chair. Ellen's body, mind, and soul are numb, as though she has disconnected from her feelings. I scream pointlessly from the depths of her body. I want to give her a voice.

"Daddy?" she whispers.

"You're not my daughter," the Miller says, as he pulls a poker from the fire place. The last thing I see before I'm ripped from Ellen's body, is the miller approaching with his weapon.

I gulp in air and am met with the dust of the Red Palace basement. Next to me, Ellen's chest heaves up and down and her head shakes from one side to the other. I hope she might wake, but a few seconds later her breathing is as measured as before.

I rub my neck. Ellen's vision had been so real that I'm still sore from where the Miller gripped his daughter. I glance down at her. For years I have been jealous of Ellen, of her beauty and popularity, and all this time she has struggled with her own secrets and her own troubles. I see her in a different light now, and I am sorry that I never stopped to wonder what the cause of her bad behaviour was. She hated herself. Perhaps we all hate ourselves at least a little bit. We're all out there right now — spread out across Aegunlund — punishing ourselves for who we truly are.

"The visions are showing me secrets," I say out loud, trying to make sense of everything. "But why?"

"Why indeed, young Mim."

The sound of his voice has me on my feet and gripping the sword at my hip. Allerton, the leader of the Borgans, and a man I almost killed, stands before me with his cat-like amber eyes gleaming through the gloom. There isn't a single hair on his head and, as always, to see him twists my stomach. This is the man who ordered the attack on Halts-Walden. This is the man who caused my father's death.

"You know my name isn't Mim," I reply, in a voice as cold as I can muster.

"Yes, my dear Mae, I do. But I thought it might grasp your attention." He giggles like a little girl and tosses the sleeves of his robes as he claps his hands together. "Oh, I am sorry. I forget that not everyone shares my unique sense of humour."

He comes to a halt at a man's distance between us and lowers his eyes to mine. I find the bile rising in my throat, longing to plunge my sword deep into his chest.

"You did this. I don't know how but you're working with the Nix," I say. "You used your amulet to curse the Red Palace and sent the court to sleep. Why did you do that? If you wanted to kill me, what was all that spiel about in the Borgan camp? That hogwash about being my mentor?" I pull the sword from its sheath and almost drop it. I'm not used to such a hefty weapon.

Allerton watches me with the sword and then sighs. "Why in the name of the Ancients would you unsheathe a sword in order to kill me? You have the greatest power within yourself! My dear girl, you have so much to learn regarding the craft-born powers. I do hope you're not going to let your stubbornness get in the way of fulfilling your great destiny."

My cheeks warm as he mentions the sword. It was a very foolish action to take, especially when I could knock him to the ground with a simple gust of wind. I consider dropping the sword to the stone slabs below, but then decide that would admit defeat.

"Why did you curse the palace? Why have you done this?"

Allerton shakes his head and turns away from me. "Why, why, why. You're asking all the wrong questions—"

I can't control myself any longer. I lunge straight for him, aiming the hilt of the sword at his head to try and hurt him, but not kill him. As I run at him full pelt, a cry escapes my lips, releasing the frustration and anger that has been tightly winding itself inside me since the court fell asleep. This causes Allerton to turn and face me just as I am flinging myself towards him. His lips twist into a smile at the very moment we are going to collide. Just as I wonder why he would react in such a way, I find myself hurtling through him and hitting the stone floor with a crunch. The sword is propelled from my hand and clatters across the ground. My cheek grazes the stone slabs, and my elbow sings from the hard knock.

"Forgive me, Mae, I should have mentioned... I'm not really here."

CHAPTER THREE

THE TORN SOUL

"You're a ghost." I push myself onto my feet and wipe the dust from my dress. "You're dead. You're a ghost!"

He chuckles and begins to stride around me in a circle. It could be the significant bump to my head, or it could be the slow, steady rhythm of Allerton's footsteps, but watching him sets me in a cloud of wooziness.

"No, no. Not a ghost. I'm still quite alive. Much to your disdain, I would imagine."

"This is more trickery. You're using my powers for your own evil gain so you can set sleeping curses and... and... walk through walls."

Allerton tips his head back and laughs until his robes shake. "I do love your imagination, dear girl. But no, I'm afraid that's not it either."

"Then tell me," I demand. "You keep saying that I need to learn, and that I can learn from you, yet you speak in riddles. Tell me what it is you want and why you're here. And please, if you can wake the prince—"

"Ah," he interrupts. "It's funny how you mention the prince first."

I twist the skirt in my hands. "Well, he is the most important person in the realm."

"But that isn't true, is it? You are far more important than any prince. You have the craft inside you. The prince doesn't even come second in this little scenario. The king, of course, is the second most important person in the realm. Unless you are a traitor? Are you a traitor?" he asks.

"If a traitor is someone who thinks the king is a tyrant and a bully, then yes, I am a traitor and I don't mind admitting it... as long as he remains unconscious." I flash a wary eye over towards the sleeping king. "The prince is more important than the king because he will rule the realm with a just and fair hand. The king is treading this world into the dirt." I twist the material of my skirt harder and harder until it forms a tight little ball in my first.

Allerton mumbles something that sounds a lot like "young love". Then he says in a louder voice, "Very well, Mae Waylander, I think it is time to refrain from beating around the bush, don't you? I'll swiftly begin. First of all, I did not set this curse. It is, however, interesting that you mention the Nix. What a horrible little trickster that thing is. Perhaps you're right about that, but we'll come to it later. Now, the reason for my current... transient form... is all down to you, my dear. As you know, us Borgans come from a long line of craft-born protectors. We worship the craft. We worship *you* in a way. We might not live as worthy believers in a monastery like the rather pedestrian priests west of the river Sverne, but we have a spirituality they will never comprehend — "

"Get on with it," I snap.

Allerton's amber eyes are hooded as he flashes me a glare. It sends a shiver down my spine.

"I am your protector, Mae, at least for now. And as your protector, I am linked to your spiritual being. That means when you are in turmoil, your soul summons me. The curse does not allow me to enter the palace, so as your loyal subject, my soul has been ripped from my body to come to your aid."

"Your *soul*?"

"Yes, dear Mae. I lay quite dead at the Borgan camp. Fortunately, I was able to forward a message to the others informing them of my departure. I'm sure they won't have burned my body." He lets out a laugh, but this time there is little humour in it.

"Will you return to your body?" I ask.

Allerton rustles his sleeves as he puts his hands together. He purses his lips and narrows his eyes as though assessing me. A strange question enters my mind: *Am I worth dying for?*

"I don't know," he answers. "This has not happened for centuries. We have written records of the craft-born going back three hundred years, and there is but one mention of a soul-tear."

"What happened? Did the Borgan survive?"

"It didn't say."

"Why hasn't it happened for such a long time?"

Allerton sighs. "A number of reasons. It takes a large amount of power to summon a soul-tear, and most of the craft-born in recent times simply haven't been powerful enough. You're different, Mae. Don't ask me why you are more powerful, because it is something I cannot answer. For a number of generations, the craft-born has lived in the Red Palace as a court member. They've lived sheltered lives where they do not need their Borgan aids. There have been some to reject the Borgan protectors all together." Allerton clucks his tongue in annoyance.

"Well, seeing as you kidnap the craft-born when she is sixteen, did you really expect anything less?"

"We don't always kidnap, dear child. It just so happens that the situation called for urgency this time around. The king was trying to marry her off to his son. We had to act fast before she was trapped." He tucks his hands into his sleeves and turns his head away. "I don't think you appreciate how dangerous this is for me. My body is left vulnerable."

I let go of the skirt and my hands flop to my side. I had no idea that my gift could do something like this. I had no idea that I could cause this. "I didn't know. I'm sorry."

"Well, at any rate. You should make the most of my presence, as we do not know when or if I will return to my body. I may be taken from you at any moment."

At one time I had wanted Allerton dead.

Somehow that seems childish now. If I had accepted my responsibility earlier on in my life, I would know how to control my powers. That could have saved a lot of people pain. It might have stopped the king dragging Aegunlund into the dirt. He has been consumed with maintaining the strange mechanisms in the castle at any cost, even the pollution of his capital city. The castle was modified to run with the craft, something that the inventor—Beardsley—created with the last craft-born.

"Now, now. You're not telling me that you are sad for me?" Allerton steps towards me and for the first time since we have met, I don't feel the urge to move away from him. "I seem to remember a rather fierce young woman with a knife at my throat."

"I didn't do it."

"No, you didn't. You're not a killer." He smiles, and this time it seems genuine. The sarcastic twitch is gone. "Now, I know you don't exactly like me, and I don't blame you. Your father was never meant to be harmed, and I'm sorry about what happened. However, I'm afraid that the world is much bigger than you and your father. It contains far more than that, and you are the centre of it all. It's a considerable destiny for one small person like you. Together we will take that destiny one step at a time."

It could be the kind words or the tired expression on Allerton's face, but I begin to soften towards the man. "Thank you," I manage.

I hear a sound that winds the tension in my body until I feel twisted up like the tree branches in the Waerg Woods. From somewhere in the castle comes the familiar *click-ick-ick-er-ricker-click-ick-ick* of the Nix, just like in my first vision with Cas.

"Do you think it's hunting me?" I whisper.

Allerton frowns and stares out towards the silent furnaces. "I don't know about that. You've faced the Nix before haven't you?"

I nod my head.

"Yes, I can see from your expression. There is no creature as despicable as the Nix. But we both know that it does not attack straight away. We are safe for the moment, Mae. It just wants you to know that it is here."

"I know," I whisper. I cannot get the thought of its black body out of my mind, or the way it showed me my greatest fear. When I had woken up with the sharp shard of stone pressed to my wrist, I had never felt so ashamed and so terrified.

"This will be a difficult fight, Mae. Do you think you are up to it?"

My fingers tremble at the thought of facing the Nix again. "If Cas needs me to do it, then I will defeat that monster once and for all."

"First, you need to move these people to safety," Allerton says. "I don't know what the Nix is playing at, but if it is trying to get to you it will use any means possible, and that includes using people you have a weakness for." He lowers his head and regards me with hooded eyes. A shudder runs down my spine as I realise he means Cas. "Is there somewhere you can put them?"

"Beardsley's room," I reply at once. "I can lock them in while we hunt the Nix."

"Mae, you won't be able to move all these people. You'll have to take the ones most important."

I stare down at the bodies by my feet. They wouldn't all fit in the office and I know it, but at least I can move Cas and his family to safety. I just have to pray that the Nix will not bother with the members of court either not familiar to me or of high importance in the realm. Even so, my throat tightens at the thought of leaving them there.

"I'll take the royals to Beardsley's quarters and then we'll just have to block the basement off the best we can," I say.

Allerton nods with approval. "Well then you'd best begin."

After an inspection, I figure out how to rearrange the tiny room to accommodate the royals. It means shifting much of Beardsley's work to high shelves and piling it up outside the door, but it gives us just enough floor space to move the sleeping bodies.

I use a coal cart to lift them, which helps a great deal. But still, shifting the king takes considerable effort, and I'm sweating and aching by the time it's done. They will have to slumber side by side until I can break the curse. It might make for an interesting awakening, but what else can I do?

After the others are safely locked away, we move out into the hallway. There, in the darkness, my fingers search the dirty alcoves of the wall for a lantern and a match. Without Beardsley's overhead lights, the castle corridors are dingy, full of shadows and stuffy. When I find the match, my hands shake and it takes two attempts to light the flame. I remove the lantern from the alcove and hold it aloft, preparing myself for the sight of the Nix.

Allerton's soul remains my one companion. I let out a sigh of relief.

"I've never seen you afraid before," he remarks. "It doesn't suit you."

"You don't even know me," I reply.

"I saw you face the man you believed ordered the death of your father without a hint of fear. I know you are brave, deep down."

I ignore him and grip the hilt of my sword in my free hand. "Let's find the monster and kill him. We don't have to talk on the way."

"On the contrary. You need to develop a plan. You will not win in a sword fight with the Nix. For one thing, you cannot swing that sword, it is far too heavy. Another thing, your powers need to develop to defeat it. I believe I am right in saying that you have not mastered fire yet?"

I attempt to jut out my chin in a confident fashion, but Allerton sees right through me.

"No, you have not mastered fire yet. Come. We must find a safe space where we can begin." He ushers me away from the long hall towards a chamber.

"Begin what?" I ask.

"Your training of course."

My jaw drops. "We can't *train* while the Nix is roaming around the castle."

"Mae, you know full well that it will not attack for a long time. Instead, as you attempt to hunt it, it will continue to wear you down with visions of fear. Before you know it you are a jabbering wreck who can't do so much as create a waft of air with your craft."

I know he's right, but still it feels wrong not to act straight away.

"You are a brave girl, Mae, but there is more you need to learn. You need to learn patience and cunning, and I am exactly the kind of person to teach you. Plus, I have a secret weapon."

"What's that?" I ask.

"I know the Nix's greatest fear."

I turn to him in shock. "You do?"

"Yes, I certainly do. Now, let's find a safe place to train. Preferably a large room with a lock."

For the first time since the curse fell on the castle, I smile. "I know just the place."

I swish my ridiculous dress as we take a left turn down the corridor. The Red Palace is an ancient castle, modified by an inventor called Beardsley. He placed strange locks on all the doors, large loops made out of brass. Each is a puzzle that fits together by sliding pieces into each other. I have lived in the castle for a little over two weeks, and in that time I have explored much of the palace by hiding and watching the others enter the different rooms. By being the eyes and ears of the castle, I've managed to memorise many of the strange combinations.

The old layout is traditional, and one I have taken interest in. Back in Halts-Walden, Father made me read books on the subject of the monarchy, and being in a place filled with history is like having a living connection to my dead father. I know that the palace is laid out in wings, with the royal chambers in the East Wing, and the guest rooms in the West Wing. Also on the east side is the ballroom, the kitchens, the engines and the servant quarters, however they are spread over three floors. On the west side there is a library, a throne room, the chapel and the medical ward, where the palace apothecary treats severe illnesses. With the servants living mainly on the east side, it is the part I know best. And I know one place where we can lock ourselves away from the Nix.

"I'm taking us to the queen's chambers," I

say.

"Well, very fancy indeed," Allerton says with a giggle. "I would have dressed up for the occasion if I'd known."

I narrow my eyes at him. "This is serious, you know. There are people's lives at stake. I need to learn how to kill that deformed slug and learn it fast."

Allerton lets out a loud guffaw that makes me start. "Deformed slug! Well I never, what a wonderful description of the Nix."

"You're not taking this seriously," I reply, turning my face away so that he cannot see my lip twitch with amusement.

We approach a large brass door covered in connecting brass rings. Each ring has to be turned into an interlocking pattern to open the door.

"Can you hold things?" I ask Alleton.

"I think not," he replies, raising the skin on his forehead that should be his eyebrows.

I place the lantern on the ground and begin to work on the lock. I have to move each ring to fit into a sequence. The sequence is marked by notches. Since living in the castle, the queen is the only member of the royal family to let me into her chambers. She had invited me to help style her hair before an evening meal. I'm terrible at any kind of hairstyling, and can only imagine that she had invited me to her chambers for the sole purpose of showing me how to enter her room. I wondered why at the time. Now I believe she predicted that something would happen to her. Why would she think that?

It is heavy work. Without the power running through the palace, I have to rely on brute force. Years of tree climbing has given me some upper body strength, but I have little weight to put behind it. Each movement on the rings leaves me with a coat of sweat on my forehead that I have to wipe away with the sleeve of my dress.

"Allerton, if I can fall through you, you can walk through walls. Why don't you go in there and inspect the chambers. The Nix could be lying in wait, and all this effort would have been for nought."

"Very well." He bows his head and moves towards the wall. I detect some reluctance, and can imagine that walking through a wall might feel very unnatural indeed. I find myself gritting my teeth as he dips a toe into the bricks.

It's with some relief that I see him disappear into the room.

"All clear," comes a voice.

With a great shove, the last ring falls into place and there is a loud *clunk* as the mechanism comes undone. Now I can press the doorknob and enter the chamber.

The door swings back with a long, drawn out creak. I hurry to re-set the mechanism, locking us in and the Nix out.

"Those locks are very curious," Allerton says. "Why would a king want each room in the palace so guarded? I know kings are by their nature a target to usurpers and whatnot, but this is another level of paranoia. Are all the doors like this?"

I shrug. "I guess so."

"Doesn't it strike you as odd?"

"This is the first palace I've been to," I reply. "Everything strikes me as odd."

The truth is that I have thought about the strange mechanisms on the doors. All I know is that the king asked Beardsley to design the palace in a very specific way. He must have a reason for doing that.

"Well, this room is large enough to begin training," Allerton says.

The queen's chambers are larger than the tavern in Halts-Walden. She has a private commode, a large four poster bed with stunning drapes hanging from each corner, and an intricate rug covering the stone floor. One wall is filled with her private book collection, which gives the air that not unpleasant must-scent from old books. There is an ornate mahogany desk and a large trunk. The wardrobe is almost the size of the hut I lived in with father. I run my hand down one of the bed posts, wondering how many queens have slept in the same bed, touched the same smooth wood.

The last time I entered these chambers I remember the queen rambling as she spoke. She sat at her dressing table and asked me strange questions:

"Have you ever wished to be a princess?"
"No, Your Majesty."
"Wouldn't you like to be queen?"
"I would rather ride Anta to a faraway land."
"Do you think you would make a good leader?"
"I... don't know, Your Majesty."
"What do you think of leaders? Do you think they are above the law?"
"No."
"Would you challenge authority if you felt they were doing something wrong, something that could put the realm in danger?"

"Yes, I suppose so."

That conversation seems far away. Long ago. I felt at the time that she was trying to test my nature, to see if I would make trouble for the castle. Now I think she might have been trying to tell me something.

Allerton paces the room with his arms folded in his robes. "I think we'll be safe here for a while. The Nix will not be able to manoeuvre through that door. At least I hope not."

"What does it want from me? Why doesn't it kill me and be done with it? Why did it show me those things?"

"What things?" Allerton sweeps across the floor, his amber eyes fiercely highlighted by the sun streaming in through the windows.

"When we were in the Waerg Woods it poisoned me and showed me a future I... I..." I grip my eyes shut. It isn't a memory I like to remember. The Nix showed how I would drift apart from Cas, become his servant, and watch him marry Ellen. In a fit of despair, I attempt to take my own life in a servant room here in the Red Palace.

"You know the Nix is a trickster," Allerton says. His voice is calm and slow. "You know that you cannot trust the things it shows you. Why dwell on it, girl? Why do that to yourself?" I drop my head as he examines me with those preternatural amber eyes. The queen's four poster bed acts as a seat for me as I almost collapse into the soft bed linen. "Ah, I see. I see very clearly and I'm not at all surprised. You hold the prince in your heart. It's a weakness to do so, of course. As protectors of the craft-born we are taught to prioritise our beliefs. The craft is more important than the heart. Your love for your father almost twisted you into a killer, Mae. What makes you think that the love for this boy will not corrupt you in the same way? Unrequited feelings are as dangerous as anger, if not more so. You could become a bitter hag, a resentful woman, instead of the powerful leader you should be."

"So the vision could come true? But you said—"

Allerton silences me with a sweep of his hand. "Pay no attention to the Nix. It is true that the Nix uses some truth, it uses our real fears and twists them. But your destiny is as fluid and turning as the River Sverne. Whatever you become it will not be down to that overgrown cockroach. Your heart, Mae...

That has a rather large part to play in your future. You need to choose wisely when it comes to whom you trust it to."

I had never thought about it like that before. Perhaps I never imagined that my heart was worth giving to anyone except Father. If I had stopped to think, maybe I would have been more cautious. It was the way Cas treated me more than anything. Despite being prince of the realm, he made me feel like his equal, and that is something I'd never known.

"It spoke to me as well," I say. "When I was in the basement, I heard its voice in my mind. It told me some sort of riddle, and then I was pulled into a vision. It happened again not long after. First there was the riddle and then it showed me a vision."

"And the visions were from the Nix?" Allerton asks, the humour long gone from his voice.

"Yes, except they were different this time. They didn't focus on me and my fears, they focussed on the fears of the others. It was Cas in one vision. He was afraid of his younger brother. The other was Ellen, who was attacked by her father. They seemed so real I felt as though I was physically hurt by it."

Allerton's frown deepens. "And what was

SARAH DALTON

the riddle? Do you remember it?"

"Yes," I say, relaying the riddle to him. "Don't you think it sounds like the answer is the Nix itself? Wearing down its victims is the Nix's specialty. Showing us our greatest fears... wait, no, it isn't the Nix at all."

You cannot touch me, but I make you cold.

"Fear makes our blood run cold. That's the answer to the riddle!"

Allerton nods. "Very good, Mae. I think you're right. Perhaps fear is the key to all this and perhaps you can use that to help break the curse."

"But why would the Nix tell me?"

"I don't know yet," he replies. "But we are going to figure it all out."

"What is the Nix's greatest fear?" I ask.

"Fire," Allerton replies.

CHAPTER FOUR

THE QUEEN'S CODE

Allerton instructs me to wash and change. My scrappy dress is torn and covered in dust. As it is a fraction too long for me, it catches on the bottom of my heels and slows me down. The thing needs to go, and not a moment too soon. Dresses are definitely not my style.

In the queen's washroom, I notice a change come over my countenance. My face is muddied from attempting to dig my way out of the castle, and my elbows are grazed from my tumble in the basement. The cuts, grazes, and dirt used to make me feel like a scrappy urchin child for whom no one cares for. Now I see them as signs of strength. Battle wounds.

The only clothes I find that may fit me are a pair of britches and boots, and a silk tunic, far too fine for the likes of me, yet somehow befitting this new confidence. The Waerg Woods have changed me. My eyes are dark and level. The restlessness has gone. My arms are roped with muscles and I have filled into a more womanly figure. I hold my chin up. Gone are the days of me staring at my feet as I walk. This is how I will hold myself from now on.

It's as though my humours are somehow coming to align. There is still the haunted shadow over my eyes, the one that carries grief. The mischievous grin—the one that always got me in trouble—has almost gone. But there's still something, a sparkle, a twinkle of the girl I used to be, the one who would joke and laugh. I like that. The responsibility I always eschewed fits well with this version of me. The weight settles on my shoulders and it is a comfortable one.

I am ready for the tasks ahead of me. I leave the washroom with my shoulders back. In the queen's bedroom we begin the training.

"It will take a strong heart, a strong head, and a strong stomach to defeat the Nix,"

Allerton says. "You need to use all the tools available to you, and you need to start using the craft as an instinct as well as a power. It resides in you waiting to be used. Bring it to the surface and see what it can do."

But no matter how his words stir me, I can't escape the churning in my stomach. Cas, Ellen, the queen, Beardsley... They remain unconscious while I attempt to create a flame in the palm of my hand.

"How is this going to?—"

"Shhh," Allerton chastises. "Concentrate."

"But—"

"Imagine you are a great furnace. Imagine the fire building inside your belly. You are the conduit, and through you, fire will come."

I try again, closing my eyes and imagining the engine room in the castle. The workers are there shovelling coal into the fires. The rhythmic chug of the shovels, the hiss of the fire, the crackle of the flames... it should rise from my gut. But somehow, nothing comes to me.

"I can't—"

"—is not a viable excuse." Allerton looks down his nose at me, with a creased forehead.

After another fruitless attempt, Allerton sighs and sits beside me on the floor of the queen's room.

"Perhaps if you understood more in regards to the origins of the craft-born," he says.

"What else is there to know? It comes from nature, from the four elements. It flows through me because I have the blood of the Ancients in my veins." I shrug.

"That's all true," he says. "But do you know how it links to the Gods?"

I shake my head. "Father sometimes spoke of them, but he was never very devout. Halts-Walden follow the teachings of Celine. Wind keeps us safe." I shrug. "The stories are nice, but we were too busy almost starving to care."

"According to the teachings of the craft, the Gods are more complex than many believe. They are not always good. They are not always concerned about the poor and helpless."

"I thought Gods were supposed to help?" I say.

"In a way," Allerton replies. "But it is more complicated than that. Long, long ago, before our kind inhabited Aegunlund, the Ancients worshipped the source of their magicks. They worshipped the four elements, not the Gods. In worshipping the nature, they conjured them in their own image. They *created* the Gods."

"Then how can they be Gods? I thought

Gods created our worlds?"

"Not this time," Allerton says. "There could be Gods who created our world, but the Gods of your powers were made *from* your powers. Celine, God of wind, Endwyn, God of fire, Ren, God of water, Fenn, God of soil. They came from the source of your powers, Mae. There is nothing you cannot change with your craft. Nothing you cannot do. The Nix has one huge weakness. Now, close your eyes and create a flame."

"Why is the Nix afraid of fire?" I ask.

"Because it is the last of its kind. A lot like you, Mae. You are born of the Ancients. *It* was born of the Ancients, too. The difference is, the Nix came from a twisted mix of beast and magic. When the craft first stirred through the veins of the Ancients it was too powerful to be tamed. It was in everything, all the elements of our world, from the plants to the clouds, and before the Ancient Ones could harness and control those powers they shot out at tangents into everything and anything. Great beasts, tiny insects, birds, men, women, it distorted them all. It wasn't until men learned to control the craft that the world began to take shape.

"Now, you see, the Nix is part of one race of creatures made from that great surge of power.

It is a monster with a brain. There is little it cannot achieve with that brain because it wears its victims down until they are nothing at all. It controls them. You've seen the way it feeds on fears. But what you don't know is that during the great Purge during Ancient times, the Aelfens burned many of the Nix's kind. Mass killings."

"Aelfens?"

Allerton tuts. "You need to come to the Borgan camp soon. There is so much that you do not know. The Ancients were called Aelfens a long, long time ago."

"Aelfen," I say, running the name over my tongue. "And I am part Aelfen then?"

He nods. "The last."

"So the Aelfens attacked the Nix's kind. But if it happened in the Ancient times—?"

"The Nix remembers. It is born with the memories of its ancestors. It remembers the pain of the fire. It has already died a thousand deaths. It needs fears of others to make it strong because its own fear is debilitating."

I don't speak for a moment. The entire history is appalling. "Is that why it's evil? Because of the pain felt by its ancestors?"

Allerton hesitates. "Perhaps."

"Does that mean it has a chance to redeem

itself? To become good?"

"Do you think that?"

I shake my head. "I don't know. I can't imagine experiencing that pain. The pain of my father's death was unbearable. It made me hard, vengeful. The thought of experiencing that thousands of time over... I'm not sure I would be me anymore."

"I'm inclined to agree with you, Mae. I don't believe the Nix has a shred of humanity left in it. I don't know why you have been targeted, but it has to be for a selfish reason."

I rub my chin, mulling over this new information. It seems more whole now, like my enemy has a face. "The court is experiencing their worst fears. It has to mean something."

Allerton frowns. "Tell me more about those visions. It could be important."

"Ellen's was horrible. I was in her body and she was beaten by her father." I decide against telling Allerton Ellen's deepest secret. Somehow it doesn't seem right.

"Perhaps this is part of the spell. Oh, that is very clever indeed." Allerton smiles. The thought that he admires the Nix is as unpleasant as the thought that each of my friends are experiencing their worst fears over and over. "A perfect way to wear you down. It knows, you see, it knows you so well. The thought of your friends facing their worst fears is more unpleasant to you than facing your own. It will wear you down until it gets what it wants."

"What could it want? I don't understand."

I stand up and pace the room.

"Mae, you really must learn flame," Allerton says in an exasperated tone.

But I am too lost in my thoughts now. There is a mystery to solve and I feel as though I must solve it before I can work on my craft. It nags at my mind.

"Something in the castle… what could it be?" I mutter to myself.

"Sit down, Mae, you're making me dizzy." Allerton attempts to grab hold of my arm but it goes straight through me. He stares at his hand in dismay. "It's very bizarre to see myself like this. I am a nonentity."

As I stare through Allerton's hand, that's when I realise that the locks on the inside of the door are far more complicated than the outside. There is another set of rings woven into the pattern with notches that are different to the exterior. I struggle to remember how the queen managed to release us from her chamber. At the time I had been dumbstruck by her questions, and so amazed at the beauty of her room, that I hadn't paid any attention.

"Allerton have you seen the door?"

"How curious." He moves behind me and his noiseless body causes me to start when he speaks. It only now strikes me as strange not to hear the breaths of a human being, or feel their movements next to your body.

"It seems the queen must be hiding something."

"What makes you say that?" I ask.

"Well, why else would she have an extra lock on her door? Either she is very safety conscious—and with that brute of a husband I can't say I blame her—or those locks lead to something else in the room."

"You mean another door?" I ask.

"That is exactly what I mean." A slow smile spreads across Allerton's features. "Let me ask you, do many people other than the queen enter her chambers?"

"Well I have only lived in the castle a few weeks but I did hear a rumour amongst the servants regarding the secrecy of the queen. They also said that she never entertains the king, that he always summons her to his chambers, and then very rarely." I feel my cheeks turn red as I discuss the relations between husband and wife.

"Well, now there could be a good reason for that," Allerton says. "Perhaps she only wants her most trusted companions to know about the extra door.

Like me, I think. She invited me here to show me, except I was too stupid to notice.

I back away from the door and begin to examine the room instead. If I was to install a secret doorway in my chambers, where would I hide it? There is the wardrobe. It seems a little obvious, but I stride up to it and work on pulling the large piece of furniture away from the wall.

"I'm terribly sorry I can't help, dear Mae," Allerton says in a voice that suggests he is not in the slightest bit sorry.

But the furniture is too heavy. I'm only able to rock it forward an inch and press my eye to the gap between the wall and the wardrobe. There isn't even the tiniest crack in the bricks, and besides, it would be useless to the queen if she had to move the wardrobe during an escape.

I work methodically around the room, removing tapestries and paintings, pulling the desks and dressers away from the wall... none reveal any secret passageways out of the room.

"There's nothing here." I wipe a film of sweat from my forehead and pant air into my lungs. "I've tried everything except…" my heart soars. "Except the washroom, of course! It's angled perfectly over the stairs in the castle, which could easily hide a narrow passageway."

I rush into the small bathroom where I had changed and washed only minutes ago. It contains a small marble basin and a large porcelain bath. I hadn't noticed anything unusual about the room before, but there is a large mirror behind the basin, which spreads across the wall from one side to the other. I place my fingers on the mirror and feel each side. The left, the closest to the wall near the stairs, has a tiny draft escaping from it.

I almost run straight through Allerton as I make my way back to the door. One of these rings corresponds with the secret door in the washroom. But how am I supposed to work out which one it is.

"Have you found it Mae?" Allerton asks.

"One of these rings will open the door in the washroom. I think the mirror is the door. I don't know which one."

Allerton watches as I nudge the rings, uselessly. There are too many combinations to

SARAH DALTON

choose from.

"How does she remember how to do this every day?" I muse. "It must be a lot to remember."

"Perhaps she doesn't," Allerton says. "Perhaps she leaves herself reminders around the chamber."

"Of course!"

I careen around the queen's large four poster on my way back to the washroom. There has to be a clue in there, something I've missed. The washroom still smells of the rose scented soap I used to clean myself, and there are small beads of condensation on the glass of the mirror. As I lean forward to examine the glass, the slight breeze tickles my ear. I put my fingers on the glass and explore the edges. It's there that I notice tiny grooves in the mirror, the same length and shape of the notches on the rings.

"Found anything?" Allerton once again sneaks up silently and causes me to start.

"There are grooves on the side of the mirror. I can't see them, but I can feel them. Each one of the brass rings has a different set of grooves. Maybe I can match them to one of the rings."

"Not bad, dear girl," Allerton says. "You've got a bright mind on those shoulders."

"Now I just need to…" I suck in air. That voice is back. The Nix.

Trailing silk, I glide, spin patterns to catch you, suck you dry.

What am I?

"Mae?"
The ground disappears below my feet. A sucking pulls me down, and the room fades away…

My feet hit solid ground. There's a clanking and hissing of the engines in the Red Palace. The air smells of charcoal and damp earth. My ears are fuzzy, as though I am hearing through water. It takes a few moments for that fuzziness to dissipate.

"And what was it that you wanted to ask me?"

I turn away from the sight of the burning engines to see an old man resting on a cane by a large bowl of soil.

"Beardsley," I say.

"You wanted to ask me something?"

"I... I don't remember."

The old man's eyes narrow and his brow furrows as he examines my expression. "You seem quite perturbed, young Mae. What could be the matter?"

"I don't know. I feel strange, like I've done this before. I... I shouldn't be here. I'm looking for something. There's a puzzle that I need to solve."

"Then you came to the right person." Beardsley's eyes shine. "I am quite adept at solving puzzles. In fact, that's what I do. I create puzzles for other people to solve. Some find it quite frustrating." His expression darkens. "And sometimes the puzzles are unsolvable. Sometimes they puzzle you."

"What do you mean?"

Beardsley shakes his head. "Nothing of any use. Now, why don't you tell me all about it?"

"Well, it's to do with the queen's chambers, and —"

"Shhh!" Beardsley lifts a hand in the air and tilts his head to one side. "Do you hear that?"

Aside from the heaves of the men working by the engines, and their voices as they laugh and joke through their work, there doesn't seem to be anything out of the ordinary. The large copper pipes hiss and clunk as the castle chugs along, surging power into every room.

"No, what is it?" I reply.

"Oh, nothing," he says, still staring out into the distance. His voice is vague, distracted. "Go on. The queen's chambers. Yes, I believe I designed the lock. She wanted something different to the king. I wondered whether it was to keep out certain members of the court. She was quite adamant..." His voice grows fainter and I wonder if he is lost in some long lost memory. "Oh, and there was the... yes, that's right... the... Don't you *hear* that demon thing scraping and clanking?"

"The engines?"

"No, you fool," Beardsley snaps. "You stupid little fool, what were you thinking? What made you think you could get away with it? Imposter!"

I step back, alarmed by this strange change in Beardsley. The man I met before seemed genial, so calm and gentle. Yet he stands before me with his mouth twisted into a tight grimace.

But as quickly as the grimace appeared, it fades and his eyes soften, replaced by the slack-jawed look of shock. "I'm sorry. I don't know... I'm not myself, it would seem."

"Maybe you should go and have a lie

down," I suggest. "Or have the kitchen staff make you a nice pot of tea. I can arrange it for you if you like. I'll go to them now."

When I turn to leave, Beardsley's bony fingers grip hold of my arm. His grasp is strong and tenacious in that way old peoples' fingers always are, as though clinging to the last moments of life. His eyes plead with mine, large dark circles of fear, black orbs within a shrunken face. The world seems to slow around us. The engines quiet. The chugging stops. In its place comes a strange breeze twisting through the room. Stray hairs are caught and pulled away from my face. Even the bowl of dirt disappears, and my stomach does a flip, confused by the sudden changes in atmosphere.

"What's happening?" I whisper.

Beardsley's fingernails dig into my skin. His mouth opens and closes but not a peep emerges. I'm about to speak when I hear the strangest noise. Around us the landscape has changed, but we are still in the palace. I can tell from the red brick of the walls, and the grandiose tapestries hanging from ceiling to floor. We are in a corridor on the East Wing. I recognise a red and gold tapestry.

"You're starting to hurt my arm," I say. His

fingers are pressed so deeply into my flesh that I imagine bruises and little half-moon marks forming on my wrist. "You need to let me go. Beardsley, can you hear me?"

There's another scrape and a loud clank. Beardsley's mouth opens and closes, his eyes are widened, frightened. His dark blue robes hang to the floor, rippling from his trembling body.

"It's coming," he croaks. "I told you it was coming."

"What do you mean, 'it's coming'? I don't understand..."

There is no point in me talking any longer, because the clanking and scraping noise drowns out my voice with its crashing crescendo.

"What is it?" I shout.

"It's coming for me." Beardsley releases my arm at last, and turns to face the sound. "I knew it would.

There's a grinding of stone as though the ground is being crunched beneath giant feet. The hallway shakes and mortar dust trickles down the walls. Beardsley backs away, bumping into me as he staggers. He stops and stands behind me.

It seems to happen in slow motion. I know I

should run, yet my legs don't want to work. My muscles tighten until they are ready to spring into action. But for some reason I cannot move. My heart thuds against my ribs, and when the hallway shakes again, I have to hold onto the wall to stop myself from falling. There's another scrape and a clank… then it emerges from the end of the hall.

A long, thin, copper coloured stick peeks from around the corner. It's swiftly followed by another one the same shape and size, then another, and another. At one point I begin to think I have double vision, because there are so many of these strange, leg-like things appearing from the bottom of the hallway. Each one scrapes and screeches against the stones.

The floor shakes as a large, metal sculpted body follows those spindly legs. That's when it faces me, and my stomach seems to leave my body. My knees are trembling, and I'm aware of the blood draining from my face.

"Mae it isn't safe. We need to…" Beardsley grabs the back of my tunic and attempts to drag me away.

The enormous mechanical spider runs towards us.

CHAPTER FIVE

THE INVENTOR'S FEAR

The scrape of its legs against the stone makes my stomach lurch. Every moment brings it closer and the *clack clack clack* of its pincers nip at my heels. My palms are slick with sweat. A desperate fear creeps up from the bottom of my bowels as it dawns on me how easily the spider could take hold of my very breakable leg with its sharp, metal pincers.

Even though I know this is one of the Nix's visions, I can't stop that primal fear from forcing me forwards. I can't stop to see if the spider will just go away on its own. I can't take that risk.

Beardsley has his robes bundled up in one hand as he shuffles along, his old legs stiff and slow. I have his other hand, almost dragging him down the corridor. The weight of the spider shakes the walls. Old shields and decorative weapons clatter against the flagstones. The tapestries fall from their hooks.

Bile rises in my throat as I think of it behind us, taller than the taverns in Cyne, wider than the farmer's cart back in Halts-Walden. Five times the size of the hut I lived in with my father, filling the great hallway of the Red Palace, and moving its many legs closer and closer to us. Those pincers...

We need to find a room to hide in, somewhere with a strong doorway that it won't be able to break through. But where?

My ankle is caught by a long, sharp leg and I cry out in pain. Beardsley manages to accelerate, his old body shuffling along the stone slabs. I push forward, determined to survive. We turn to the left, ducking down a set of spiral stairs, hoping the change in direction will slow the spider at least a little bit. I'm breathless and Beardsley is weak, but we hurry down the stairs as fast as we can. I glance back and see the spider struggling to negotiate the steps. Its eight legs tangled and squashed into the smaller space. The change in direction helps us put some distance between us, and it is distance that may save our lives.

On the floor below, Beardsley points one bony finger towards a door on the right, protected by the interlocking brass rings. I nod, and together we work the rings. Beardsley knows the combination immediately. I wonder how many secrets he keeps for the royal family, and importantly, from each other.

Inside, I realise from the large four poster bed and ornate dressing table that we are in the chambers of the queen. I'm back here again, but this time there is no Allerton. Somehow the vision has led me here. There must be a reason for that.

"What *is* that thing?" I ask.

Beardsley wipes sweat from his forehead and half collapses on the bed. "I... I designed it. The king wanted me to design a weapon more fearsome than any other in Aegunlund. That's what I made for him."

"For the love of the Gods, Beardsley, did you have to make it so big?"

He shakes his head. "I've made worse for the king. I help him do worse."

I don't like the haunted expression in the lines of Beardsley's eyes. I move towards him with the intention of saying something comforting, or putting a hand on his arm to calm him, when there's a sickening crunch. A high-pitched screech, like the sound of a pig in pain, comes from outside the room and a shudder ripples through my body.

"Is that the... the thing? Can it screech like that?" I say, backing away from the door. Beardsley comes to my side.

"I designed it to be controlled by a master. But... but I fear it has a mind of its own. That's what I've always feared." His voice shakes.

There's a great screeching noise as the spider attempts to make its way through the brass door. The metal against metal is deafening, forcing me to clamp my hands over my ears. But then there is a crunch and a scrape. The pointed leg of the spider slices through the door. The spider attempts to retract its leg, but becomes stuck against the metal, screeching in panic.

"We need to get out of here!" I yell.

Beardsley rushes towards the washroom. "There's a way out, I built it. But the combination is on the door."

I falter for a moment. "I... I... need to know the combination. That's it! That's why I'm here."

The spider manages to release its leg, but now it moves to the door, forcing its pincers through the gap left by its leg. The pincers gnash and clank, eating at the metal.

"We need to be quick. Beardsley, what's the combination?" I wrench an ornate sword down from the wall of the queen's bed chamber and inch towards the spider, jabbing the sword in its direction. I'm no master of swordsmanship, and find myself wishing that Cas was by my side. At least he can swing the damn thing.

"Oh, now, let me think." The old man rubs his chin with trembling fingers. "It was a long time ago. There are many, many doors."

The spider forces more of its leg through the gap. It thrashes around, flopping up and down until it breaks an ornate dressing table in two. I watch in horror.

"You knew the combination outside right away. You can do this," I encourage.

"Go to the door. I'll remember as I see it."

I make my way towards the door, ducking and dodging the great brass leg of the spider. Its pincers clack and grind through the door, and I jab my sword at it, trying to force it back. There are great glassy expanses where its eyes should be. Perhaps if I can jab through one of those sockets... I force my way forwards, swinging the sword. I connect with the metal leg of the spider and sparks fly. It does no damage to the spider, but the vibrations pulse down my wrist, jolting my arm.

When I'm in front of the door, the spider reaches for me with its pincers, but the door holds. I arc the sword and deliver a blow on top of the pincers. It manages to dent the metal very slightly, but my wrist sustains a worse blow. I yelp and almost drop the sword.

"Beardsley, you need to tell me, now!"

"Oh dear. Oh the Gods. I'm not sure I... hold on. Are there three brass rings?"

"Yes!" I shout. My heart surges with fresh energy. I duck and swivel to the right, narrowly avoiding another attack from the spider leg. It crashes down on a chest and fine dresses spill out onto the floor.

"Let me think. The left one works the door, the middle section is for the connecting doors to Prince Casimir, oh yes... it's the right ring, Mae. But I can't remember... the notches are supposed to match up."

"Beardsley! You need... wait." A memory pops into my mind, one where I run my fingers down the grooves of a mirror. Yes, there were notches on the mirror and they were designed to match up with those on this ring. Of course!

I steel myself and turn to the brass rings. We

don't have long. The spider has managed to force two front legs through the door, and both of them are aimed towards me. I'm able to swing the sword around to stop those powerful legs coming down on me, but I can't stop them forever.

My fingers trace the notches on the outer ring. They need to be turned to match the inner ring, I remember now. I remember the pattern. In order to move the rings I have to lean most of my weight against them.

I let out a frustrated growl at how stiff the rings are. It takes all my strength to move them the smallest amount. With the continuous crunch of the door as the spider forces its way in bit by bit, I can only put my head down and work as hard as I can.

"Mae. Watch out!"

Beardsley's cry comes too late. One of the spider legs hits me on the side of the head, knocking me to the floor. As I try to stand, it grasps me with both of its legs, lifting me high in the air. I wave my sword around, trying to find a place to hit the spider, but the metal appears impervious. I feel helpless. I can only jab and jab at the legs, sparks flying; metal clashing against metal.

"Mae!" Beardsley calls out. "Hit the eyes.

They are the weakest spot."

But I am too far from its eyes to land a blow. I have to wait, suspended in the air, for it to decide to either drop me or bring me closer, all the time, those pointed legs dig into my sides, bruising my ribs.

"I can't... I can't reach..."

Beardsley comes charging forwards, moving with speed and determination. He shuffles quickly across the stone floor with his eyes set. Gone is his haunted expression. This new Beardsley seems younger. His energy gives me a new hope.

The bony fingers that had not long ago gripped my arm, now take hold of a large, heavy looking candle stick. He climbs onto the bed, gaining height on the mechanical beast. With one swing of his arm, he lands a hit right in the centre of the spider's eye.

The sudden blow shocks the spider, causing it to drop me. I land with a thud, hitting my shoulder with some force. I cry out, but do not waste any time on the floor. Instead, I am up and limping to the door. We have managed to prise a little time out of the jaws of defeat, and now I *need* to open the trap door so we can escape.

Another notch falls into place. This time

Beardsley helps me move the ring, but with my limp arm, it is still tricky. The spider has backed away, dazed by Beardsley's destruction of one of its eyes.

"Just one more notch," he says, his voice strained and tired.

We put both of our weight behind the push, forcing the stiff brass rings into action. Sweat forms by my temples and my body is hot with the effort. Beardsley wheezes, clutching his chest.

We are almost there, with the last notches lined up perfectly, when the spider charges at the door, hitting it with full force and pushing its pincers back through the hole. This time, it connects with my side, ripping open a wound that gushes with blood. I stagger back, my eyes wide and fearful.

"Mae!" Beardsley stares at me in shock.

"Don't," I say. "Just open the door."

He nods. There's a sad look in his eye, but I have to ignore it. With one last shove, the ring is in place. I hear the sucking sound of another door opening.

But the spider is not long behind. Beardsley hurries towards me, pulling me away, but not before I see the spider burst through the broken pieces of the door. Within seconds, its enormous body fills the chamber. It screeches, and steam pours through the pincers. Beardsley's grip on my tunic is strong as he forces me into the tiny washroom and, finally, into the open tunnel. Once inside he pulls a stiff brass lever and the heavy stone door closes behind us.

The screeching and scraping of the spider seems far away now. Instead, our laboured breaths are the loudest sound in the dark, damp tunnel. We are safe, but the blood still pours from the wound at my side.

The lantern casts long shadows against the dark walls of the tunnel. It winds down, following the path of the stairs. But there are tunnels that lead off in alternate directions. This is more than an escape route, it is a maze of hidden rooms and walkways. My heart soars as I wonder if there is a way out that has not been cut off by the curse. Deep down I know it is unlikely, but there must be a fleeting chance that the Nix forgot something. Perhaps I can find help. Can I do that when I'm inside Beardsley's fear? I don't know, but it's worth a shot.

"So your worst fear is the thought of being attacked by one of your own inventions," I say.

Beardsley sighs. "I wish it was that simple. I have many fears. When you get to my age they build up like belongings. Some revolve around my inventions and what they will do to me. Some focus on what my inventions will do to others. They have already caused so much trouble. If I hadn't let the king convince me to run the castle with coal, the city of Cyne would not have perished. The farmers pray to the Gods for my great demise. I swear sometimes at night I can feel them. I sense their loathing."

I swallow thickly and press the strip of Beardsley's robe against my wound. It is painful, but the dizziness is worse; as though at any moment I will slip off into sleep and never come back.

"I feel like I can't leave you yet. I feel as though there is more I need to know, something in regards to the Red Palace. You have a secret, don't you? Something you won't tell anyone?"

Beardsley's back stiffens. "What makes you think that?"

"I don't understand why you're scared of your inventions hurting people, and yet stubborn regarding your secrets. Have you ever thought that maybe I can help?" I say.

He shakes his head. "The things I have done..."

"Beardsley, focus. You need to tell me what you've done."

But his eyes are lost in the depths of the shadows. I'm not convinced that I will be able to obtain anything of any use from him now.

"At least start with the tunnels. Why are they here? What do they lead to?"

"The queen," he says. "She always knew what her husband was. She always suspected he was rotten inside, a brute. She wanted a fail-safe for her family. She wanted to be able to escape the Red Palace. They are secret, very secret. The king never comes to her chambers, always sends for her instead... it was safe there."

"What was?"

"The passageway, of course. And the watching area. You see all the secrets there." He sighs again. "He never knew about her secret door. I built one for him, too. But he never knew about hers."

"What?" I ask, frustrated now. "What do you mean? What secrets?"

"All the secrets..."

Beardsley's voice begins to fade away. My

ears are foggy. The world begins to blur.

"No," I shout. "No, I need to know more first."

The sucking sensation takes me over, pulling me down into the ground. It's like I'm falling and I'm helpless. Another voice: *Mae?*

In one instant, I see a shape, a very sharp, very clear shape that I recognise immediately. It is the Nix.

I don't see it in the castle corridors or even in the Waerg Woods. I see it surrounded by light, but I can make out every part of its features. From the deep black shells on its body, to the lumpy long neck and fat thorax, to the long legs that scuttle when it moves and the mouth filled with pointed triangle teeth. It is waiting for me. I can feel it.

We will meet soon, craft-born, when we are both ready. There's something I need you to do for me. If you help me, I will help you, too.

"Never," I whisper. "I will never help you. I'll die first."

The ground is hard against my shoulder blades. My head is sore. My shoulder is sore. My side is sticky and wet.

Mae?

I feel as though I am being pulled from one dream to the next.

"Mae. You must wake. You're bleeding"

I see the amber eyes first, then the shiny bald head. "Allerton."

"Yes, yes, it's me. But first, you need to dress that wound. I cannot do it for you because I cannot lift."

When I sit up, a searing pain rips through my side. "It can't be," I mutter. "But it was the mechanical spider. I never... I was never supposed..."

"Mae, quickly, put pressure on the wound. You have lost a lot of blood."

No wonder I felt woozy when I was with Beardsley. I reach for something nearby that might help stop the bleeding, the best I find is a blanket from the queen's bed. When I tear strips, my stomach sinks. If the king finds out I have destroyed his property, he'll have my head. But I don't have much of a choice, it's either this, or watch my life-blood seep into the stone floor of the castle.

I wrap the strips of blanket around my wound. It is deep, but not as bad as I had imagined when fighting the spider.

"What happened?" I ask Allerton. "How did I obtain this wound? In the vision I fought a spider. But it was just a vision."

"I watched you writhing on the floor,

unconscious yet mumbling the name 'Beardsley'. The wound appeared in a sudden slash as though you had been caught by a sword."

"It was no sword. It was the pincers from one of Beardsley's inventions."

"Who is this Beardsley?" Allerton asks with a frown.

"He is the designer of the castle. In the vision he told me the combination for the ring on the door, and we went into the tunnel behind the washroom. There is more in the tunnels than we think. He said there was somewhere to watch and find out all the secrets from the palace."

"I don't like the sound of this," Allerton says. "Secrets sound like something the Nix would be interested in. As the most powerful creature in the Waerg Woods, it is always looking for ways to increase its power."

I tie off the blankets over my wound. It smarts, but I am able to stand. I stagger over to the door to inspect the brass rings. A flash in my mind reminds me of the sickening crash as the spider's legs broke through the metal. It makes my stomach lurch all over again.

"You need rest," Allerton says. "You should sleep. I will try to wake you if I hear the Nix.

Otherwise, we are safe here."

There's a burning curiosity inside me. I want to be back in the tunnel, exploring these secrets Beardsley talked of. But I know Allerton is right. I have to rest if I am to carry on. I climb onto the queen's bed, no longer caring if my blood seeps onto her sheets.

As I am drifting into sleep, I say aloud, "The visions pull me in whenever they feel like it. I don't... I can't seem to be able to control them. And they are all so different. Sometimes I am aware, sometimes I'm not. And, if I can be hurt in the visions, that means I can die in them too."

CHAPTER SIX

THE WEIGHT OF RESPONSIBILITY

I wake to find Allerton sitting on the floor with his eyes closed and his legs crossed.

"What are you doing?" I ask.

"I am communing with my body, dear girl." One eye peeks open to reveal the pale orange beneath the lids. "I wanted to check in and make sure it's all right."

"Is it?"

"Everything appears to be normal, yes." He opens both eyes and stretches out his legs. "Even as a mere soul I seem to experience the aches and pains of middle age. Perhaps it reveals the power of both habit, and the mind. How is the wound healing?"

"Well," I say. "When I was in the Waerg Woods with Sasha, she said that I heal faster than other people. Is that because of my power?"

"Of course it is. Nature responds to your cry for help. It fills you with whatever you need to become well."

I pat the bandages thoughtfully. With my craft abilities I rely heavily on nature. But what does my existence mean to the world? Sometimes I feel like a tornado-like force, sucking energy from everything around me. Other times I am a hurricane, blowing power outwards into the realm.

"It takes time to come to terms with the craft, Mae," Allerton says. "When this is over you need to come to the Borgan camp and learn more about what you are. As a group, we have been studying your kind for centuries. I may personally have never worked with a craft-born like yourself, but there are older members who have. There are books and teachings. There's much to learn, if you open yourself to the thought of learning."

My muscles instinctively clench as I remember my breakdown in the camp. It was the moment I accepted my father's death. I cannot think of the camp without letting grief back in. Yet I know he is right, and there is a part of me yearning to discover more about who I am. I just need to learn to distance my painful memories from the thought of Allerton. I need to see him as a man who made the wrong decision, not as the man who was directly responsible for my father's death. Can I ever manage that? I'm not sure.

"I don't know," I say softly.

"Mae. You are young and you wear a heavy crown. You must come to study your craft."

"A heavy crown?" I repeat.

"The crown of responsibility, dear. Every craft-born wears it. You wear it heavier than the king, I dare say. His is a bejewelled imposter, but yours is real. It doesn't fit right yet, but it will. Trust me."

There it is. The word that hangs between us. *Trust.* A word that is earned through actions. There have been so few positive actions between myself and Allerton, that I am unsure if trust can ever blossom. We started in the worst possible way—from rage and hatred. I am trying, but it is harder than anything I have ever tried before, and I am new to trying, new to growing, and new to friendships. I turn away from him and stare at an ornate tapestry on the wall. It depicts the crowning of a young prince: Ethelbert the Third, if I remember rightly from my father's books. I have seen a sketch of the tapestry in the books. Father would be proud to know that I am in its presence. A twinge of pain crosses my heart. Perhaps it is my injury that is wearing me down, but I cannot ever imagine a friendship with Allerton. Deep down I still blame him.

Allerton lets out a long sigh. "You will learn to trust me. It will take time. I wish we had more time to bond, but I am afraid that we will never have enough. All I can do, is show you that I am here as your guardian, in the same way your white stag is."

"Anta?"

"Yes, dear. He is a protector like I am. He has watched you since you were a baby, and I am sure there is something of the Ancient spirit inside him. The beast is a magical one. I'm almost certain of it."

Pieces begin to fall into place. I always felt safe and calm around Anta. He has been a constant in my world. He has always been there for me, even when others are not. Of course he is magical. That's why the villagers were afraid of him. They felt it. They felt the magic in me, too. That's why they have always been wary.

A deep sadness tugs on my heart. If that is true, everyone I ever meet will feel that same wariness. They will harbour a deep suspicion, even if they don't know why. All my life I've hidden a secret, and believed that I've hidden it well. Now I know that isn't true. They all knew. Everyone I've ever met has always known. I'm different. They just don't know *how* different.

"Is it possible to sense magic?" I ask Allerton. "When I meet other people, do they know what I am?"

His eyes half close in thought. "Yes, I think they do sense it. They might not know *what* they are sensing, however. I certainly felt your power the moment I saw you." He regards me for a moment. "You feel alone, don't you? That's the crown, my dear. That loneliness is its weight." He moves closer to me and lifts a hand as though to place it on my own. Then he thinks better of it and tucks it back into the sleeves of his robes. "As there is only ever one craft-born at a time, you will never quite rid that feeling of loneliness. But it is important for you to know that you are not alone. The Borgans are here to—"

"The Borgans are forced into protecting the magic for the realm. It has nothing to do with wanting to be around me. You're *obliged* to be around me."

"And what a great honour it is. You're special, Mae."

"Because of the magic, not because of me, not because of my character or beauty, because the Gods know I have little of both," I say, without meaning to sound self-pitying. It's a fact as plain as day. I could choose to ignore the fact I am not beautiful, but somehow that isn't in my nature. "Even the prophetess from the Ibenas said I was a normal girl, that there was nothing special about me apart from the magic."

Allerton straightens his back and frowns. "And do you plan to let a mentally ill teenage girl speak for who you are and who you intend to be? Because if you do, you will never become anything of any merit. Is that what your father would have wanted?"

My head snaps up. Hearing him mention my father brings some of the heat back into my veins, leftover anger from the grief I've carried for weeks.

Allerton purses his lips. For a fraction of a second, I think he is hiding a smile. It's as though he wanted to anger me. "Ah, now that's the Aelfen spirit."

"The Aelfen spirit?" I ask.

"Yes, that's right. The Aelfen spirit. Your ancestors, dear. They were a fractious bunch. Even before humans invaded Aegunlund there were wars between the tribes. Territory was important to Aelfens, but even more important was a sense of loyalty. If that loyalty was broken, their tempers flared. Oh yes, they were a race who saw very little middle ground, moral to a fault."

"Do you think I'm like that?" I ask, thinking of my desire for revenge after father died, and for the way I struggled to see the perspective of the Borgans.

"Who knows," Allerton says. "I don't believe we are defined by our blood, at least not in an absolute sense. Our surroundings have as much impact on us as anything. As do those who factor in our lives. Perhaps there is a little of the Aelfen hot-tempered morality lurking within you, but mostly I see a girl who observes and learns."

I open my mouth to speak, and then pause. I've never felt as though I fit in with the people around me, which means I've never figured out how I'm built. This one nugget of information is like a huge piece of the puzzle being put in place. Sometimes I feel like a broken vase that must be mended bit by bit. Whether I trust Allerton or not, I know that he is right when he tells me I need to learn more about my ancestors. I need to know what it is to be craft-born.

"Shall we open that tunnel now?" he says.

My stomach growls as I climb out of the queen's bed. I'm still in the bloody shirt from the night before and I head into the washroom to change my clothes. The dressings will need to be changed and I should check the wound on my side. I'm relieved to see there is no infection, and I find proper bandages in the bathroom. Then I take another tunic from her majesty's wardrobe and hope that she does not have my head on a spike for theft.

Before leaving the bathroom, I run my fingers over the notches, memorising their size and frequency, before heading back to the door. The loops face me. I shudder at the memory of the mechanical spider lunging through the door, its pincers biting into my side. I shake the memory away and work on the rings, bringing the symbols together. When it's over, the mechanism gives a quiet click, and a cool breeze spreads through the chambers.

"You did it, Mae," Allerton says. He nods

his head as though impressed.

"Beardsley helped in my vision."

Allerton's impressed expression fades into a frown.

"What is it?" I ask.

"It could be nothing," he says. "I just have a bad feeling in regards to those visions."

We head into the tunnels, pulling the lever to close the entrance. The lantern is in exactly the same place, and I light it and hold it aloft. It is exactly the same as in the vision, so alike that it is uncanny.

"Beardsley said there was a viewing place. That there was something I needed to see. What do you think that means?" I say. "It has to be connected to the queen in some way. There must be a reason for her to have a secret door to this tunnel. Beardsley adapted the old castle and used his inventions to customise it to how the king wanted it. He said the queen asked for these specifications in her chamber. He said that he presumed she wanted an escape route for her family. But why would she keep it from the king?"

"Perhaps she is afraid of the king," Allerton suggests.

"That makes sense, he is scary. But he is the father of her children. Why would he hurt his own children?"

"Why do men do anything? For money or love, and I can't imagine that man loving so much as a kitten, let alone his own children. I imagine he could stamp on a disabled duckling and feel no remorse."

I try to hold back my chuckle but fail miserably. "He would have us beheaded if he heard us. The first thing he did to me was shoot me with an arrow."

Allerton chuckles this time. "Imagine if he knew the truth. If he learnt that he had shot the craft-born with an arrow... after his utter obsession with finding the craft-born... well. What a fool he is. If there is one thing more dangerous than a tyrant king, it's one with an empty head."

We press on through the damp tunnels. The mouldy stench drifts up to my nostrils as I walk, turning my empty stomach. How long has it been since I ate? The memory of steak pie and chocolate cake makes my mouth water. We should take a detour to the kitchens soon. Perhaps there is something untouched by the curse that I can eat.

"Do you know where you're going?" Allerton asks.

I'd been following the same path I walked

with Beardsley in my dream, but now we came to the point where the vision had ended and I'd been brought back to the queen's chambers. It was here that we talked of the king, and of how Beardsley has done bad things for him. My gut tells me that there is some significance in the words Beardsley said to me.

The things I have done…

All the secrets…

And these things he has done, they were for the king, for something he requested. If the Nix is showing me the vision, and then *inside* that vision Beardsley brings up the king, then surely the king is the key to all this? But the other visions showed me different things, like Cas and Ellen and her father… all of them seem to involve bullying in some way. My head spins as I try to make sense of it all. There is no sense.

"This is as far as we came," I say. "I don't know where to go from here."

"But you know the basic structure of the castle. You can follow the tunnels in a general direction. This is where you begin to use your instincts, Mae. You must call on your powers to help."

"Then I think we should go to the king's chambers. The palace designer mentioned something in his vision and I want to follow it up. He mentioned secrets. Also, he said that both the king and the queen had secret doors leading to the tunnels. Perhaps I can find it."

We hurry on, negotiating bends and twists. Three times I have to stop and think. During my time in the Red Palace I have explored almost every nook and cranny, but I have not been *inside* the king's chambers. I've been near them, and I've quizzed the poor waiting staff who deliver his breakfast every morning, but I've never been inside. My palms tingle with anticipation. I'm ready to learn more about the king and his motives for the castle. I want to know why he wants the castle running on magic. There must be a reason, and Allerton is right, it has be to do with money or power, or both.

As we follow the tunnels, which dip and rise between stairs, sneak between walls and duck underground.

"I think we're close," I say, squinting through a thin gap between stones. "That is the corridor next to the king's chambers. If we take a left here… yes… here it is. Another door! And the lever is in the same place." After a tug on the lever, the wall scrapes sideways, revealing an entrance into the king's bathroom, in exactly the same place as the queen's. "Both the king and queen have matching hidden tunnels without either of them knowing. Can you believe that?"

"I can. Court members like to keep their ears to the ground and their eyes hidden in the shadows. Perhaps the queen has been spying on the king," Allerton suggests. "She would want to keep *that* secret."

My pulse quickens as we step into the king's chambers. It's one thing entering the queen's room when I know she would treat me kindly if she knew the circumstances, it's a different matter when you know that the king would have you executed without a second thought. This is real danger now. I am risking everything for more information. I hope I find something to fight the Nix.

It is a vast chamber, and as flashy as you would imagine. The king has spared no expense when it comes to his own comfort, despite the hungry families we passed on the way to Cyne.

Luxurious silk drapes hang from ceiling to floor. Unlike the rest of the castle, these are clean and new. The stone floor is covered in deep, soft rugs that feel spongy underfoot. His bed is huge, twice the size of the queen's bed.

His desk is a behemoth of wooden architecture, stacked high with papers. It seems strange that out of the entire castle, the king would work on business matters in his personal chambers, but that might be an indication that he has business he would prefer to keep from his confidantes.

The room is not unlike the others in the castle, but there are slight ornate touches on the arcs of the windows and the sills. It strikes me as typical of the king to want his room to be better than any other, that perhaps his sense of worth lies in the way the world perceives him as a man. He wants to be someone who is above any other person. While I could feel pity for a man like that, I have a scar below my ribs that only reinforces a bubbling hatred worming its way within me.

I travel across the room, idly nudging papers and books to see if there is anything worth looking at, only to find a long, vicious whip. I lift the whip at the handle and examine it. An image flashes into my mind, the king bent over Cas, whipping him. Cas has never mentioned being hit by his father but I doubt a man like him could resist beating his children. Heat rises as my rage builds, and I drop the whip to the floor.

"Mae, dear girl, what is it we're looking for?" Allerton asks. His eyes travel from the whip to my empty hands.

"I don't know." I sigh. "Instinct told me to come here, but it has left me now. I don't know what I'm doing. What would the Nix want from the castle? Why am I the only one not asleep?"

"Slow down, Mae. Think of what you *do* know — not what you don't know — and then we can fill in the gaps as you work everything out."

"I know that everyone is asleep. I know the Nix is here in the castle. I know that my powers can't break the spell, and I keep being pulled into visions. The first one showed me Cas as a little boy, hiding from his brother and afraid of his father. The next showed me Ellen who was beaten by her father. Then I met Beardsley, afraid of his own inventions. He helped me solve the brass rings on the queen's chambers."

"What does all that tell you?"

"That the visions are important. The king is bad. Beardsley made something for the king that he's afraid of —"

"There!" Allerton claps his hands together. "That is the key. If Beardsley created something for the king that he's afraid of, it must be important. And if it is important, it is something that the Nix might desire."

"So I need to find whatever it is that Beardsley has invented. But how?"

Allerton shrugs.

"And that means the Nix is sending me clues in my vision. Wait, no. Not necessarily. It was only in the vision with Beardsley that I received any kind of clues, at least that I'm aware of. Apart from the riddles." I groan. "This is so frustrating."

"The Nix is a trickster. He likes to play God with his subjects. He wants you to question what you believe. He wants to confuse you as much as possible. It's how he weakens his prey, by working at destroying your mind."

"Well, I won't let it," I say, attempting to dismiss my worries and focus on what I do know—there are secrets in the castle and if my conversation with Beardsley is correct, they lead back to the king.

I set to work on the desk, rifling through the documents. Most are bills of some kind. There is written evidence that the king has sent a vast amount of money to Jakani, but that he owes even more.

"Could this be to do with diamonds?" I ask

Allerton. "There are rumours in every tavern in Aegunlund that the king makes illegal diamonds to sell in Jakani. They say the great Jakani mines are drying up, and the slaves are dying under the sun."

Allerton places his hands together like a steeple. "That would certainly fit into the money and power spectrum. The Red Palace is in disrepair and he needs his jewel exports in order to recoup costs. If there is some sort of treaty with Jakani for diamond production, perhaps that would account for the tension in Cyne."

"I don't know," I say. "It's hardly a secret, and it doesn't explain what Beardsley is afraid of."

I keep digging through the papers, uncertain as to what I will find. What I'm doing now could be seen as treason and my throat tightens at the thought of the possible consequences.

"Wait, what's this?" I pull a wide sheet of paper out from under the pile. On it there are diagrams, jotted numbers, and an invoice of some kind. "These sketches are like the mechanical spider that chased us through the castle. And below... look, here." I push the paper under Allerton's nose. "It's a command to all the blacksmiths in Cyne to make these specifications." I tut. "He's paying these people a pittance. It's little more than slave labour. Father earned pennies less than that trading wood at the market."

Allerton shakes his head. "He's a tyrant king. But why would he be building such a large quantity of weapons? If the man is making money with the Jakanis, why would he need to create an army?"

I read more of the paper in front of me. "This command demands complete secrecy. Anyone caught talking about the weapons will be sentenced to death! That's what it says here. Something strange is going on. It looks as though the king is financing weapons for an army.   But ·   why?"

CHAPTER SEVEN

THE ALTERNATE PERSPECTIVE

Even Allerton remains in quiet contemplation as I search the rest of the king's chambers. We find no more information regarding the large order of weapons or the mechanical spiders. There is nothing that details plans by Beardsley. I can't imagine who the king intends to attack with his army. For all we know he could be stockpiling the weapons for a later date. Perhaps he is waiting for an attack from someone else. My mind immediately goes to the Jakanis. They are the most hot-blooded of the people in Aegunlund with their many mines and slaves. They dominate the salt and diamond trade. I can imagine the king wanting control over their riches, especially with Cyne in such disarray. But as far as I know, the king needs the Jakanis on his side, he needs their money. None of this makes any sense.

Allerton continues with his lessons. The Nix often fights his battles in the mind, but it is still a large physical presence, and if I am to destroy it, I must use all my powers. But no matter how hard I try, I can't seem to make the flame appear in my hands. However, I have learnt to create a small tornado, the size of a book or a plate, and I can control its course. Wind seems more drawn to me than any other element. I can't help thinking that it matches my personality. I am not cold or hot, I am forceful, wild and untamed.

"Very good, Mae. You are able to control wind with your mind. From my readings, many craft-borns have found this to be the hardest."

"What about fire? Did they find fire the easiest? Why can't I conjure fire?"

"That depends on the craft-born's heart. Those who are hot-headed and easy to anger usually do well with fire." He laughs. "That gives the Borgan protector a lot to handle."

"But I've always been easy to anger," I say. "Why can't I do it?"

"You've been through a great loss," he says.

"It could be the grief you feel for your father that has changed your heart. Are you still easy to anger?"

"I've gone through many changes since Father died. I don't know anymore. I don't know who I am."

"Do any of us?" he replies. "I'll let you into a secret that you learn as you get older. None of us really know what we're doing. We just muddle along the best we can. The person who tells you they know everything is a bare faced liar."

I let out a sigh. It pains me to say it, but I must. "Maybe the reason I can't create fire is because I'm working with the man who killed my father."

Allerton's eyelids droop and his jaw slackens. He seems more resigned than I've ever seen him. "I can't change the past, dear Mae. One day, I hope you will believe how sorry I am."

I shake my head, thinking back to the time in the tent when Allerton had seemed conniving, cold and tricky. Even though he is now with me as a protector, I cannot shake the unease his presence brings out in me. And if I can't ever shake that unease, how am I supposed to work with him? After all, I have not just myself to think of, but Cas and the rest of the court. "Why are you my protector? Why can't it be someone else?"

He pauses and looks me up and down. "Well, I'm certainly the most able from my camp. I am the Borgan with the most knowledge. I have studied more books than anyone else. But it would seem that, despite being the best at what I do, and the leader of the Borgans—by *appointment* I might add—that our first meeting is something that we might never be able to overcome. Will you see me as anything but the monster who caused the death of your father?"

I ruminate on that for a moment. "I'm trying, but I don't think I am ready yet."

The words hang between us. They create a wide gap, a distance.

"Why don't you use it?" he says with pursed lips.

"What?"

"Use the anger you feel towards me. You can't hurt my soul. Use it on me. Set me alight." His amber eyes flash with wicked mischief.

I suck in a deep breath and stare at Allerton, imagining the first time I laid eyes on him. I remember it as though it had happened just minutes ago. He had walked through the Borgan camp with a line of guards. I watched with the hatred burning in my stomach, knowing full well that those guards were the same men who ransacked our village. They killed my father so they could kidnap the craft-born. On *his* order. Allerton. I was supposed to be taken, but instead they took Ellen. And in the fighting they killed the one person I love in this world. They killed the man who raised me and looked after me and taught me how to behave.

For the first time since I watched the flames lick the sky during my father's funeral, I feel the heat rising from my belly. I concentrate on that heat, building it up to my chest, but as I begin to let it consume me, an image of Cas's face pops into my mind. We sit by the campfire talking and laughing. I see his gentle nature and it makes me want to be better. It makes me want to be better than vengeful. The heat dies and I slump.

"I can't."

Allerton frowns. "Idiotic girl! Don't you see that you will put lives in danger if you cannot get angry enough to use the fire element?"

"Can't I defeat the Nix another way? Why can't I do it with wind?" My breath comes out in rasps. A slick of sweat forms on my forehead. I must have used more energy than I had imagined. Now, I feel my arms and legs begin to weaken, and the desire to lean down on the cold stone floor of the king's chambers. The familiar fade takes me over and the room begins to darken...

...and the voice comes...

What lasts a lifetime but takes a moment?
What resurrects those who have gone?
What remains as a mirror image in the mind?
What is different for others but the same for you?

I'm sucked down into a vision.

Pine and birch. I know the trees simply by inhaling their earthy, sweet, spicy scent. The air is familiar. It's home. I open my eyes and see twisted branches, feel the mud on the forest path, and hear the thundering noise of horse's hooves.

I dive out of the way, missing the hooves by a hair's breadth. A gasp escapes my lips as I curl up into a ball. When the hooves sound further away I open myself and sit up. In the clearing of the forest a chestnut mare comes to a halt. Two other horses stop behind her. The first rider wears a cape. He has sandy-blond hair.

Curious, I climb to my feet and step forward. There's something familiar in regards to those horses and their riders. My hand rises to my mouth in shock. A dark skinned short girl stands next to the chestnut mare. The sight makes my blood run cold. That's *me*. And I know that boy... it's Cas. This is the exact moment that we met.

"What does it look like? I fell," says an irritated voice. My heart sinks. That is *my* voice? Is that how childish and insolent I sound.

"You Halts-Walden folk are strange," says Cas. "And rude. Is that how you address your prince?"

The other version of me lets out a curse. I notice the slight wariness in her eyes as she tries to compose herself. She is afraid, so small and afraid, and yet naïve, too. She does not know that within hours Father will be dead. My heart pangs for us both. "Sorry, um, Your Majesty."

"Highness," he corrects. "Well, that's quite the worst curtsey I've ever seen in my life, but I suppose it will have to do. I must confess that we're rather lost and late. My guard saw a rare white stag and we thought to hunt it. Father would be so impressed to mount the head of a—"

"How dare you." The version of me standing in the mud clenches her fists in fury.

The prince's jaw falls open. "I beg your pardon?" As the prince's skin prickles with annoyance I realise that this time I am connected to him, too. I feel what he feels, see what he sees. He's curious about the girl below him. He wants to learn more, but he's irritated by her, too. She gets under his skin with her attempted wit. At the same time, he thinks of her like a wild animal: a wild cat who does not want to be tamed and who is treated with wary respect.

"How dare you hunt my stag?"

"I'm sorry, your stag? Surely you don't *own* the stag." He moves his horse closer and stares down at her with a curious expression on his face. I remember how at the time I thought he was pampered and entitled. Now I see him as interested and inquisitive. "*You*."

"Yes, he is mine, so no one touches a hair on his head, or I kill them."

The guards begin to unsheathe their swords,

but Cas stops them. It pains me to see them again. I remember their mangled bodies in the tavern. Poor Cas. They were his friends. I was torn apart by my own grief, not realising that he was also in pain. It's like a revelation to recognise how our own pain blinds us from the pain of others. I hope I never let that happen again.

Why am I being shown this scene? Even though I've lived it before, I see it from an alternate perspective. This time I'm closer to Cas. Even though I am not in Cas's body, I see me through his eyes. I've always been confused by Cas. He always treated me as an equal, which is something no one else except Father did, but at the same time I was either an annoyance or his friend. Now it seems as though I am interesting to him. It's as though he has never met anyone like me before and wants to know what makes me the person I am.

"No, it most certainly isn't. Thank the Gods. I wouldn't swap places with that ninny for all the sticky pastries from the bakery."

The prince shares a glance with his guards. "Are you saying my future bride is a ninny? She's not... She's not ugly, is she?"

I remember how Cas's words had annoyed

me. He'd seemed shallow and overly concerned by the superficial. This time I see a young boy terrified by the prospect of marrying a stranger. When I hid my craft from the villagers I did it because I was afraid of marrying a prince I didn't know. Why shouldn't Cas have been just as frightened?

"*Stout?* Oh Gods above, she's a pig, isn't she? Father assured me she was the most beautiful girl in the village. But, well, no offense, but looking at you hasn't given me much hope."

This is the moment where he made me feel ugly. Cas clearly thought I was plain the moment he saw me. But now, when I see me through his eyes, I don't get that impression. Now, I understand that he was trying to save face, and that he didn't think I was ugly at all. In fact, there's a slight twinge of heat in his cheeks, as though he feels exactly the opposite.

How strange.

"Some people think that a person's personality is what matters."

"Does she have a good personality then?"

"Oh no," I reply. "She's horrible."

I cringe at my own words. I am childish. Such a fool. Instead of traipsing through a muddy forest in my mother's dress, I should be spending my last hours with Father, appreciating him and everything he did for me. Instead I annoyed him with my disobedience, and I caused him to be angry with me for the rest of the day.

I'm pulled out of Cas but remain in the Waerg Woods. The riders move away and I feel the prick of tears in my eyes. I want to scream at the Nix about how pointless this is. Why is it showing me my first meeting with Cas? What does it mean? More importantly— can I trust it at all?

Instead of being sucked back into the king's chambers, I sit down in the grass of the Waerg Woods, contemplating the scene I've just witnessed. What if the Nix is trying to distract me from my task? I can see how this would be tempting, watching a Cas who appears to like me from the very beginning. But then, what would be the purpose? The Nix has trapped me in the Red Palace for a reason, and it can't be to moon over a boy I can never have.

Unless the Nix has no control over the fears of the people he has cursed. I know that the visions are our own fears brought to life, rather than a prediction of the future as I once worried. What if these visions are the same? What if I—somehow—have to overcome the fears of each person in order to break the curse?

I climb to my feet in excitement. For once I have a clear plan. If I can learn to control the visions I am sent to, perhaps I can change the outcome of whatever it is the Nix wants to happen. The problem is—I have no way of knowing how to do this.

A low moaning sound, deep like a wounded animal, erupts through the air. My muscles respond at once.

"Anta!"

I would know his cry of pain anywhere. I rush through the forest, tripping on my dress. In that instant I am back in the moment I first rushed away from my father, worried for Anta, worried what will happen to him. He's my guardian, according to Allerton. He has been sent to protect me, to help me grow into a woman. Memories flash through my mind as the branches of the Waerg Woods scratch my face—Anta as a foal, staring in through the window, as a calf when I was a child, lowering his head so I could slip onto his back, then later, riding furiously through the woods, free as a bird.

"Anta!"

Another call rips through the forest. What

was once the brightness of midday has turned to the dark of night. When I move through the trees, I see little of the path. My aching muscles force me to slow down, and once or twice I trip and fall into the nettles below. My hands sting from their bite but I do not care. I push forward, terrified of what I will find, but terrified to turn back and leave him alone.

I slow until all I can hear is my own breathing and the snapping of twigs. Where am I? I could be close to the deadly fog, or the vines that suck blood, or the Nymph. I could be anywhere. I press on, shifting obstacles out of my way as I search for my one true friend.

A low moan. So low and tired that it frightens me.

With trembling fingers, I part the branches of a bush and push through the foliage. It's there that I see him, nestled in the fallen leaves. I drop to my knees at his side, my insides turned to water from fear. Fear of losing him. I forget the visions in that moment. It is only me, and my one true friend, a pure innocent being who should never be hurt like this. Anta's breath exhales, warm and foggy into my hand. He nickers to me. And then I feel the warmth of his blood. It's everywhere, seeping into the muddy floor of the forest, spreading thick and fast over his coat. I can't find the wound, but I know deep down in my heart that he is badly injured, that he could...

CHAPTER EIGHT

THE LITTLE PRINCE

Anta.

Before I even have time to cry his name, I'm sucked into the king's chamber. The smell of the king's cologne mixed with ink and leather filters through my nostrils. The ground is hard beneath me, and my palms tingle with a spreading soreness. Allerton's voice seems faraway, like a whispering ghost.

I sit up straight. *Anta.* What happened to him? I wipe the sweat from my forehead with the back of my hand. Why did I find him alone and bloodied on the floor of the forest. That isn't what happened after I met Cas and took him to Halts-Walden. Later that night he had been hurt, but only by a stray arrow; never hurt to the extreme I saw in the vision.

Had the Nix included my own fears into Cas's vision? It made no sense.

"Mae? Are you all right?"

I stare at him, and then I stare down at my sore hands.

"Nettle stings. That must mean it's real. It's real!" I rush to my feet. Allerton regards me with eyes wide with panic.

"What is the matter, Mae?" He implores me with arm gestures.

"I have to get to Anta." I move towards the door to the King's room and begin working on the brass ring. It's no use; I don't know the combination.

"Mae, what are you doing? You can't go out there, the Nix—"

"He has Anta!"

"Calm down and tell me what you saw in the vision this time? You know that you cannot trust anything shown to you by the Nix, you know that."

I ignore him and hurry back towards the open passageway. But then I think better of it and shake my head. It would take too long to travel back to the queen's chamber, and if I try to find an exit elsewhere I run the risk of getting lost within the twists and turns.

"He must have a clue somewhere." I carry on going through the King's belongings, no longer caring whether he will find out I have been in his room. I pull the papers and books to the floor, rifling through them with manic ferocity.

"What are you looking for?" Allerton demands. He stands by me with his mouth hanging open.

"Anything I can find to help me end this. The Nix wants something and if I find it I can finish this once and for all."

"Mae, you need to tell me what you saw in the vision. Take a deep breath, and talk to me," he says.

But the panic has taken me and I can't see straight. I hear the riddles going around and around in my mind, feel Anta's blood on my hands, see Cas's silver eyes staring at me. That memory has taken me straight back to the girl I once was, has torn open a wound I thought had healed. There are tears burning behind my eyes.

"Mae," Allerton says. His voice rises in frustration. "Stop ignoring me. I must know what has happened. Why are you panicked? Are you letting the Nix in? Are you letting it rile you?"

"No," I reply, moving around the room, tipping papers and clothes to the floor.

"You're lying. You need to focus."

"No, I need to help the people who need me."

He stands and watches me as I try to avoid his amber eyes. He is powerless and we both know it. Without a corporeal form he cannot force me to do anything.

"I'm not sure I can be your Protector," he says after a pause.

I stop what I'm doing and turn to him. "What are you saying?"

"I can't help you. There is too much bad blood between us and I will not gain your trust in the short time we have to kill the Nix. I feel that I am hindering your ability to progress. You cannot open up while I am here. Look at you, clearly terrified by something you have seen, and yet unable to talk to me. I cannot get through to you."

I open my mouth, feeling as though I should say something to contradict this. I have nothing. He's right.

"I should leave," he says. "Let you figure this out on your own."

My eyes widen. "You're leaving me alone?"

He shakes his head. "You're never alone. I

will be watching you. I will be there if you need me."

"But you said that you're not my protector."

"I can still watch over you," he says mysteriously.

"Will I be alone here?"

Allerton doesn't answer. Instead, he fades.

"Wait," I say. "I…" I know I should tell him to come back.

"Goodbye, Mae, I'm sorry," he says, slowly fading away.

I watch him dissipate from the room like wafted smoke, with a heavy feeling pulling at my heart. I should shout that I didn't mean what I said, but part of me wonders if he is right. How will it ever work as guardian and craft-born if I cannot trust him? I run my hands over my bare forearms, rubbing the warmth back into them. The empty room has caused the hairs on my arms to stand on end.

The last vision frightened me more than any of the others. I don't know whether it is because it concerned the people closest to me, whether it is because it brought me so close to the home I once had, or whether it is because the Nix has worn me down, but my mind is more fractured than ever. I am desperate for this to end.

I have to concentrate on getting Anta back. I'd assumed him safe and well outside the castle in the King's stables. Now I know that no one is safe. I can't stay locked away from the Nix forever. I have to stop hiding in the royal quarters. It's time to face my own fears.

I examine the King's desk for clues. The queen had her combination hidden within the mirror in her bathroom. The king might have a similar code. His desk seems to be the main focus of the room. I imagine that he loves this desk and loves the sense of power it gives him. It is very much like him: flashy and brutish. I run my fingers over the surface before trying underneath, feeling the lip of the wood for any clues. It's smooth.

But when I pull out the drawer, I notice that it doesn't seem quite as deep as it should be. It's there that I notice a tiny version of Beardsley's brass locks, but this time without as many combinations. Can I be lucky enough to guess the combination? I finger the brass ring, hidden at the back of the drawer under a pile of papers. A man like the king must have many hidden compartments, all locked away by Beardsley's locks. There's no way he could remember so many combinations. I pull out the drawer below and feel along the edge. Yes!

There! Just like with the queen's mirror, the king has had subtle notches carved into the wood. This time I am taking no chances. I might one day need the combinations. I take a piece of paper from the drawer and begin to write down all the combinations to the doors I know in the castle, before folding it and placing it in my britches pocket.

Opening the secret compartment is easy now. When the fake bottom of the drawer pulls out, I find only one item hidden away: a small notebook, approximately the size of the holy books in Halts-Walden, thick and chunky, but only around the size of your hand. I lift it out and flip open the first page.

I am in despair.

It appears to be a journal penned by the king. It begins with those morbid words. This is not what I expected at all.

I need Beardsley to rid me of this fear once and for all.

I refrain from reading further. Aside from it feeling too personal, it's strange, to the point where I wonder if he is in his right mind at all.

I don't need to know the mad ramblings of a despot king. What I need is the combination to his chamber so I can leave. I thumb quickly through the pages and come across the jackpot on the inside flap of the final page. The king has listed a number of secret combinations to doors inside the Red Palace. I place the notebook in my pocket and grab a new sword from the wall. It is lighter than the last sword, and when I test it against my forearm, it is sharper too.

With my new tool, opening the door of the king's chamber is simple. Soon enough, the last notch falls into place and the mechanism clicks open. I grip the handle of the door and hesitate, the weight of being alone settling on my shoulders. I never thought I would miss Allerton. Yet I do. I roll those aching shoulders, check the wound in my side—a dull background pain now—and examine my red hands. I cannot keep falling through these visions. One of them will kill me. No. Enough is enough. I am going to face the Nix head on and end this once and for all.

I swing the door open wide and step into the corridor.

It is silent.

Whether I expected the great, slithering bug

to be waiting for me, I'm not sure. But I pull in a deep breath of relief and say a silent prayer that I did not come face to face with my enemy before I am prepared.

I calm my pounding heart by pulling in a few deep breaths and then slink around the corner, holding the sword aloft. I know Allerton says I should use my powers, but there is reassurance in the chilled steel. It is heavy in my hands, but I like that reminder. The engraved hilt reminds me of Cas and my heart tugs. I would love him to be by my side asking stupid questions. I miss the sound of his voice.

A thick silence hangs in the air. I hear no tell-tale signs of the Nix. In the Waerg Woods the Nix scuttled through the paths with its large, slug like body, and the plates of its back clicking together. That noise is the one thing that slips into my dreams at night. It is the one thing that has been left to me from the Waerg Woods. The only other image that comes close to haunting me is the thought of Finn struck through the chest by the prophetess.

I gulp.

Where am I going?

I move swiftly through the castle, walking on the balls of my feet, placing them softly against the stone slabs. Somewhere a door creaks. Could it be caught in a breeze? Or is it the Nix catching up with me? Perhaps I have made a mistake. The last vision has messed with my mind, forced me into making mistakes. I shake the doubts out of my mind and move on.

It's time to decide on how to act. I need to hunt the Nix once and for all. I have to make sure we all survive this. Fear niggles at my stomach. I haven't mastered fire. According to Allerton it is the one thing the Nix is afraid of. But he's gone. He's left me, and I must do things my way.

The stairs disappear beneath my feet. My breath begins to pant as I pass the kitchens and head for the engines in the cellars. I know this place all too well, now.

As I lift an arm to wipe the sweat from my forehead, the familiar sucking sensation rips me from the corridor.

"No," I whisper. "Not now. No!"

I devour hearts.
I am in your worst fears.
I am in your brothers and sisters.
I am in you.

Have you solved my riddles yet, craft-born? Or is the uneducated peasant girl struggling with the big words? You need guidance. Let me guide you. Let me lead you…

I'm back in the queen's chambers. In my hand is a needle and thread. In the other is a swatch of material, embroidered into a delicate pattern of roses. The sun is shining outside. I rest on the window sill with my knees up. I am balanced against the barred window, staring out at the city before me. It's a beautiful sight. The tall shop buildings are brightly painted, pastels and reds and brown, dotted with signs and slogans. Beyond that I see the ploughed fields of the farms. Some are patterned with crops, other are still dirt brown. Further still stretches the green fields of Aegunlund, merging in with the darker green of the long forests. The north is famous for its green pastures, and so it should be, they are magnificent.

Back I go to my humming. I work the needle in and out, in and out of the material, building the soft pastel greens of the leaves. This will be a fine addition to my collection, perhaps the most perfect of them all. I've learned an abundance of skill since the days when mother would chastise me for my poor technique. I take in a long breath, remembering Mother is a difficult task. My heart twists both out of love and grief, and bitterness and hatred. She was a cruel woman, obsessed with her daughter's success yet jealous of it at the same time. Alas, my corset is too tight to allow me that sigh.

"Mummy, Mummy, look what I can do."

I turn my head to the sound of the voice. The sight of his sand coloured hair always fills my broken heart with such joy. Casimir plays on the wall of the opposite side of the castle. At once I drop my embroidery to the floor and get to my feet. He is high above on the ramparts.

"Casimir, stop that at once. Climb in through the window!" I wring my hands, agonised at the sight of my child in such a precarious position. "You must stop!"

"But Mummy, Lyndon said you would be pleased."

At six and four, Casimir, despite being the oldest, is by far the most naïve of the two. Lyndon seemed to come out of the womb a calculating old man. He was a longer baby than Casimir, and a greedier baby, too, and he remained taller than Casimir as he grew.

"No, Casimir, I am not pleased. I'm not angry, but you must turn around and move back to the window. Do it now, darling."

My heartbeat quickens and I place a hand over my chest. Where is Lyndon? Why has he told Casimir to do this? He may only be four years old, but there is something worldly about him. I fear it is to do with how much time he spends with the king. The man is a bad influence.

Casimir takes small steps towards the window and my heartbeat begins to calm. When he is safe I will run to him and scoop him up and smell his hair again. The absence of him in my arms makes me ache in the bottom of my stomach, an ache that longs for another baby. That ache will go ignored. I will never bring another child into the world, not when the father of that child is the king. If I'd known then what I know now...

With a jolt, I realise that the dark head of my second child waits for Casimir at the window. Lyndon stands, oddly tall for a four year old, waiting for his brother.

"Lyndon, move away from the window and let Casimir back into the castle," I shout through the bars of my own window. They are easily wide enough to let a small child like Casimir through.

My muscles begin to clench. Lyndon has a

smile on his face that lifts the hairs on the back of my arm. I send a prayer up to the Gods.

"Lyndon, help your brother back into the palace. Lyndon, do this or Mummy will be cross." I back away from the window, ready to sprint to the other side of the castle. If anything happens it will be too late. It is too far to dash across. "Guards! Guards! Help my son." I know it is useless to call for the guards. There are so few of them now. "Finan! Help us, Finan!"

Lyndon reaches his small chubby arms through the bars of the window. Casimir is crying now. He realises what he's done and he is afraid. My heart twists at the sound of his voice. It is too much. I have to go to him.

I turn and run through the room, turning in the direction of the crying. On the way I stop and stare out of the window. I don't have as good a view as in my room, but here I can see Lyndon's arms moving towards Casimir.

"That's it, help your brother," I call out in my most soothing voice.

I'm about to move away in order to continue across to the boys, when I notice Lyndon's hands. They are not open as though to take Casimir's hand in his, they are flat, as though he intends to push him.

"Lyndon!" I scream. "No!"

The scream that leaves my body ripples through the castle like a strong gale. I collapse in on myself, my knees buckling beneath me. With one hand, I grasp uselessly onto the bar of the window, as though I can still reach out to him. I will never smell his hair again. I will never feel him in my arms again. I will always see him, falling, falling...

Small footsteps tip tap along the castle stones. A tall child appears around the corner of the wall.

"Why are you sad, Mummy? I will be king now. Isn't that what you've always wanted? Daddy says so."

I wake in a pool of sweat. Thank the Gods, it was just a dream. Still, I think I will check on the boys.

As I plan to leave my bed, I become aware of someone else in the room.

"Casimir?" I say. My voice is a whisper.

"No, Mother, it's your second choice."

My breath freezes in my throat. "Lyndon, my darling boy—"

"Save it," he says, in an ice cold voice. Lyndon has never been an affectionate child. There has always been a sense of disconnection in the way he interacts with the world, but this new tone is different. It frightens me. "I know what you think of me. I know that I am not your favourite. I don't think you even like me. Daddy liked me. Casimir hated me. Maybe it was because I stabbed the whining boy with a sword, who knows."

My voice trembles. "What do you mean... hated?"

Lyndon tosses two heads onto the bed as casually as if they were bread rolls. My second scream of the night rips from my body as though someone has reached down my throat and dragged it out. Without a second thought, I swat them off the bed and crawl up until my knees are under my chin. My son and my husband. My son. Dear Casimir. My Cas. And I swatted him away like a bug.

He died a violent death.

The pain is too much. I am broken.

"I'm going to be king," Lyndon says. "As soon as I've got you out of the way." He lifts a bloodied knife and the moonlight catches the blade. A manic grin reflects in the steel.

CHAPTER NINE

THE HUNTRESS

I suck in air as I wake, with tears running down my face. It was the worst one of all. I *was* the queen in that vision. There was nothing I could do to change it. I felt so helpless. I had felt the pain of a mother whose son had killed his sibling. I saw her entire world crumble in one, awful moment.

My throat burns with held back sobs. I rub tears away with my sleeve. The poor woman. Of all the fears I have experienced, hers is by far the most disturbing.

I lift my head and try to compose my thoughts. The Nix taunted me before this vision, taunted my ability to decipher his riddles. Well I know this one; I knew it immediately, like I knew myself. It was evil. Pure evil. But still, my mind is in a spin. None of these visions make any sense. Am I supposed to take something from each one? There is only one thing that connects them all, and that is fear. Ellen is afraid of her father finding out her secret, Cas is afraid of his brother, Beardsley is afraid of his inventions, and the queen is afraid of her youngest son. But out of all the visions I have walked through there is one that stands out. The vision in the Waerg Woods where the Nix replayed a memory, but showed me Cas's side instead. Why would the Nix show me that?

These visions are needlessly confusing. If the Nix wanted to kill me, it could have jumped out from behind a corner and squirted me with its serum. The Gods know that last time I almost finished the job myself. Yet so far it has remained hidden. It is tormenting my mind instead of my body. That is why I must seek it out myself—before I lose my mind.

As I pick myself up and continue on my task, I can't help but wonder if the king is secretly plotting to secure Lyndon on the throne. If he is, that would mean murdering his own son, and he would have to do it before

Cas married Ellen. The king still believes that Ellen is the craft-born and his plan is for the future queen of Aegunlund to be the craft-born. Perhaps that would explain why Beardsley is filled with regret. Maybe the king has conspired with Beardsley to kill Cas.

Surely he couldn't do that. I won't believe it. But I can believe that it is a dangerous time to be the king's least favourite son *and* the heir to the throne. When I break the curse I must warn Cas, or the queen, that I suspect foul play. I feel sick at the thought of Cas being in such danger. The sight of him murdered… it was too much.

Every muscle in my body shakes from fear and weakness. I need to find food before I hunt the Nix. I'm dehydrated and my stomach growls angrily. Keeping my back to the wall and silently moving my feet, I tread softly through the castle. The kitchen is on the level above.

The kitchens are eerily silent. I'm used to the cook being there to shoo me away from her stew, or rap me on the knuckles with her wooden spoon when I try to steal a pastry. My heart twists to see her slumped over the long table, her arms hanging down loosely. At least the spoon is still in her fingers. I help her onto a chair, and then do the same for the staff. At least then they won't hurt themselves when they wake.

I swallow. *If* they wake.

For the first time since the curse began, I find myself considering the fact that I might lose. After all, the odds are stacked against me. I am just one girl who cannot use her powers to their full potential, or fight well with a sword. I cannot see anything consistent within the visions for me to be able to fight through them. What will happen to all the innocent people locked away in Beardsley's room? Will they just die? Will the Red Palace remain under the curse for years to come? Aegunlund will be plunged into chaos without the security of the royal family. I might hate the king and all that he stands for, but to have no one on the throne would be worse. Who knows what kind of fighting might break out, or what kind of tyrant might claim the throne?

My burden seems to increase a little at a time, bit by bit, until my back doubles over with the weight. I have a choice—I can shoulder this burden, lift my head up and keep going, or I can buckle under it. I'm not prepared to buckle under. I refuse to see innocent people suffer. Allerton was right about many things.

The kitchen is not cobwebbed like the rest of the castle. There is an undeniable stillness, and when I knock a pan to the floor, the clatter causes my muscles to tense up and my heart to pound. I reach down, replace the pan back onto the table, and continue into the larder.

While I've never been allowed into the larder, I know this is where the cook stores supplies for the castle, and I know that this is the most likely place to find food. My mouth waters at the sight of fresh bread and cooked meat. I hurry back into the kitchen in search of a knapsack. I settle on an apron, which I can tie up and loop over my back. On my way back to the larder I spot a punnet of fresh strawberries and pop one into my mouth. The juices are delicious.

After a meal of bread, ham and cheese, and after I've filled the apron with slices of cooked meat, bread and fruit, I loop the straps over my shoulders and under my armpits, securing the food on my back. I gather a few extra supplies, like matches and candles. I lift up the sword and practice a swing. With my stomach full and my thirst quenched—I sipped on wine from the larder which both warms my blood and pulses courage through my veins—I am ready. This time, I know I can defeat the Nix.

It's time to hunt.

As I stalk the corridors of the Red Palace I think of the times Father took me hunting. I was always a bad hunter. Too impatient, I would startle the prey by hurrying towards them with my bow and arrow stretched. More often than not, I released the arrow too quickly, alerting rabbits and deer to my presence, while missing them by an arm's length.

Father said it was because my heart wasn't in it. When we practiced with bottles in the woods, I hit the target dead on. But when it came to taking a life, I always missed. He thought that my heart ruled my head, forcing me to make a mistake and spare the animal's life. After that, I let Father hunt and I cooked instead, nursing my wounded pride. I always considered it a weakness, and indeed, I tried to keep Cas from noticing my reluctance to take a life. It was only when Sasha brought it out into the open that I was forced to acknowledge it.

I cannot let that weakness resurface when I face the Nix.

As I've travelled the length of the East Wing, logic tells me that the Nix must be hiding somewhere in the West Wing. I set off in that direction, gripping the hilt of my sword. This time I can't miss my mark. I don't have anyone here to help me, not even Allerton. I can't hesitate. I can't scuff my heels against the stone floor, or drop a bread roll. I must stay alert. I must be ready. My skin tingles with anticipation, and my recent meal gurgles in my stomach. What if I don't have the heart for it?

I focus myself by thinking of Anta in my vision. This one felt different. It felt as though Anta saw me, really saw *me*. I could be wrong, of course. It could be the Nix trying to mess with me. That's how it works after all. It wears you down until you can't fight anymore, can't think anymore. It was a warning. It had to be. If I close my eyes I can feel the warm blood dripping through my fingers. He is in danger, and when Anta is in danger I run to him without hesitation. This is no different. Only this time, I have a curse in my way.

Somewhere in the west of the castle comes a sound. It's faint, but a thud followed by a scuttling noise. I freeze. My pulse quickens and I move back against the wall, lifting my sword, listening.

Silence.

After a few moments, I press on, moving gingerly, catlike. I'm aware of my breaths and the slight film of sweat on my palms. I adjust my grip, taking care not to drop the sword.

Never before has the tiny scrape of my shoes against stone sounded so loud.

Clickerickericker-ick-ick.

The Nix! I spin towards the noise, but am faced with nothing. I can no longer control my breaths, they become ragged and laboured with fear.

Ick-ick-click-click.

As soon as I hear those sounds I am back in the Waerg Woods. The memory of the sickly coating of its serum on my arms and legs is real enough to cause me to check I am still unhindered.

Those terrible visions flood my mind: a servant to Cas, unequal to him as he becomes king, melancholy and lonely as I attempt to take my own life. I had wanted desperately to leave that vision. I resolved to disappear from the Red Palace and travel down to the Haedalands to allow him to live his life with Ellen without my interference. Now, as I hunt the Nix, that's all I can think about, how I still might become the woman in my fears.

No. This is what the Nix wants me to contemplate. It knew all this time that I would never be able to stay with Allerton, and it knew that I would be alone. I am not strong. I am weak, and I let my own fears swallow me whole.

I lift my sword and move forwards. The East Wing is long and winding, with many unused rooms to pass. But I head towards the library in the west, passing slumped guards and dusty tapestries. The light streams in from the narrow windows, picking out tiny specks of dust suspended in the air, and highlighting bright squares on the floor.

The noise comes back, but this time I am ready for it.

"Your clicking doesn't scare me anymore, you overgrown slug!"

My voice echoes through the winding corridors of the castle.

Click-ick-icker-ricker-ick.

That scuttling sound never fails to make the hair stand up on the back of my neck.

I steel myself, lifting the sword aloft. As I walk towards the sound, I calm my breathing and think of wind. I must make sure my powers are at the surface if I am to fight.

Craft-born, you do not need to be scared, it says. *That is not the purpose.*

"Then what is? Tell me what you want."

A sick chuckle ripples through my mind. I want nothing more than to clamp my hands over my ears.

Telling you would achieve nothing, craft-born. You will retrieve what I want regardless. You will have to.

"Why?"

I step around another corner, expecting to see the sight of its enormous black, slithering body. There is nothing to see.

"Why?"

That laugh comes back and it makes me gag. I've never heard a laugh dripping in such malice. The evil almost seeps through my heart.

I cannot take this anymore. I have to finish it once and for all. When another turning becomes fruitless, I break into a sprint, running as fast as I can towards the library.

"What are you going to do to Anta? If you harm my stag, or Cas, I'll kill you!"

More laughter. This time it doesn't sound as though it is in my head. It is coming from the right. I change direction and follow the sound. As I pass old paintings of the royal family, and dusty suits of armour, the sword weighs down my arms until the muscles ache.

"Come out and face me, you coward!" I scream.

All in good time, craft-born, it taunts.

That's when I realise that I'm being tricked.

The Nix has planted the sound of its laughter in my mind, and while I've been chasing it through the hallways, the Nix has gone in a completely different direction. I swear under my breath and turn back. Where could it be?

I have to take a risk. If I cut through the library and run to the left, maybe I can cut the Nix off as it moves through the West Wing of the castle. It must be heading in the opposite direction to me. It might not work. For one thing, the Nix might have turned off along the way, but it is the only thing I can think of.

I grip the hilt of the sword and enter the library through the great wooden doors. It is a large, tall room with a mezzanine floor and a balcony overlooking the stacks. Normally I love the sight of the library, it reminds me of Father teaching me to read, but now I am tensed, coiled like a snapped whip, my knuckles white and my throat dry. Yet I concentrate. As I stalk through the quiet library I think of wind. I focus on howling gales and twisted tornadoes. I imagine the doors on the opposite side of the library and the corridors beyond. I can send two gusts of wind coming from either side to trap the Nix somewhere along the hallway, giving me an advantage.

It takes much of my attention to summon

wind and run at the same time, and as I cross the room my mind slips into a dangerous wooziness that I have to pull back. With a shake of my head, I manage to keep myself together. One of the tornadoes rips ahead of me, churning the castle in its wake, shredding a tapestry as it travels.

I hurry along behind with my sword lifted. There is no longer silence in the castle and the clicking noise of the Nix has ended. Out of the library, I take a right and follow my creation. There is little I can make out through the wind, but I keep my eyes on the lookout for a large black shape. Surely even the great Nix will be hurt by the searing strength of a tornado.

I duck to dodge a flying piece of debris as I move forwards. The tornado answers my command when I force it on faster, like a loyal dog. I put both hands on the hilt of my sword, knowing that we must be close. My heart pounds with anticipation. This is it. This will be the moment I defeat the Nix.

A sickening squeal rises above the sound of the wind. I rush on, bursting through the tornado, which doesn't touch or hurt me. However, a flying silver jug hits me hard on the shoulder.

When I see it, my blood runs cold. This is

the first time I have faced the monster since the Waerg Woods, and all the taunts, riddles and sickening laughs spin around in my mind as fast as my own tornado. For a horrifying second I am petrified by its presence. The Nix has reared up and is being buffeted by the wind. Its many legs wave in the air and its jagged teeth gnash together. As its body bends, the hard shells on its back clack together, as though it is made of more teeth; teeth and shells and squidgy underbelly. The eyes hold mine, a translucent green over blackness. At the sight of me, it squirts out its defensive serum, but the wind sweeps it away from me.

Using more of my power, I create a mini hurricane to dislodge some of the bricks from the surrounding walls, careful not to take too many. There's a rumble as the bricks fall from the walls, hitting the Nix in all directions. I stop quickly, in case I bring the palace down on us all.

You are not as powerful as I am, craft-born, it taunts me. *Where is your white stag to protect you now?*

At the mention of Anta, I lunge forward and stab at the Nix. But too late I realise this is what it wanted all along. In the midst of tornadoes and bricks, the Nix is able to strike me with one of its long, pointed legs, and it scratches me all along my face and down my chest. The shock causes me to fall back, and it's then that the Nix sprays its serum over my body.

Whatever you see, he will never love you. It will not be because of the craft-born imposter, it will be because you lied to him.

You will break your heart in two.
I'm always wrong and so are you.

"No!" I cry out. It's no good. I'm sucked away, sucked back into a vision.

It's Cas again. His eyes have lost the swimming tears of the young boy I saw at the ball, to be replaced with the contemplative melancholy of adulthood. Yet, as I watch him by the window of the bell tower standing out towards the sea, he reminds me more of that boy than of the Cas I know. I think of the queen's worst fear and my heart hurts. I've watched him murdered twice. The pain had been to the point of unbearable, and not just because I had felt the queen's emotions, but because when he hurts, I hurt.

He speaks. He does not know I'm here.

"What am I going to do?" he whispers. "Mae. Mae, what am I going to do?"

He shakes his head sadly.

"I'll never love her."

"Never love who?" I shout. I rush towards him, desperate for him to see me. "Who will you never love?"

I'm a ghost in his world and I always have been. I'm desperate for him to see me. It's not a thing that I can prove, it's just something that I know deep down in my bones: I have always been the ghost in his world. A spirit of a girl. A spectre to haunt him. My heart has never felt so raw, and so swollen.

I reach out to touch him. He bows his head and grips the sill of the open window. The cool breeze coming from the sea lifts his hair, and it ripples down to the collar of his tunic. I long for him to turn his silver eyes towards me. Just one more time. One more.

I imagine them damp with tears.

Well this confirms it. He must be talking about me. He said my name. Cas will never love me and had may as well move on with my life. At least now I have the confirmation I need.

But as I turn away from Cas, the world

shifts once more. I'm sucked away and pulled into another scene.

I'm back at the ballroom. The quiet solitude of the bell tower has been replaced by the bustle of gowns and the thumping of the orchestra. It's a fast tune, one different to the slow melody played at the last ball. My chest is constricted once more, proving that I am squashed into yet another uncomfortable corset. When I lift my hand to the chill on my neck, I discover that my hair has been braided away from my face, and a mask has been clipped into my hair, covering my face. But apart from that, I am me. My skin is still dark, I stand in an unladylike manner, and my mouth waters at the sight of the food.

Perhaps I have been sent back to the same ball I saw the young Casimir at. With a sinking realisation in my stomach, I realise that I could be here just to watch Lyndon kill Cas for a third time.

But then the room spins. My feet move in time to the music, and I am swept away by a dancer. It is as though I have done this before, and my body already knows how to react. If I am in someone else's fear, that must mean I am myself, but playing the part of myself in their vision. I gaze up at the high ceilings. There are banners and bunting hanging from the chandelier. They spin and spin above me as I dance around the room.

My partner is tall and wears a mask which conceals his features. There is some sort of gauze obscuring the colour and shape of his eyes. The mask disguises the view of his hair, too. But his arms are strong and he moves well across the floor, even when I trip. I am not a good dancer, but it doesn't seem to bother him. He pulls me a little closer, until there is only a finger's breadth between our bodies. It is perhaps a little too close for polite society, but again, my partner does not seem to mind at all. He appears quite at ease with the dance and the ball in general. His clothes are fine. The tunic is embroidered with gold thread. He must be extremely wealthy.

It's only then that I look down at my own gown, expecting it to be made out of cheap fabric and ill-fitting. It is not. It is a beautiful white gown with delicate flowers stitched in silver.

"You dance well," I say. The words spill out of my mouth without any thought.

"As do you," he replies. His voice is stiff and stilted, as though he is nervous.

I relax into the dance. Before long I enjoy the

twists and turns, and the way my dress sways with my body. My partner's warm hand rests on the small of my back. His touch is a comfort to me, something I can relax into, and with each lap of the dance floor we move closer until our noses are a hair's breadth from each other. We're verging on scandalous, but I don't care any longer. I am consumed by the thought of his arms around me and the desire to rip away the mask. I long to reveal his eyes, to know this man.

"Perhaps we should get some fresh air," I suggest. Again, the words come from my lips, but I have little control over them. It is as though I am acting the part in a play, controlled by some puppet master somewhere. The Nix?

"That sounds agreeable," he says.

We break from our embrace, with some reluctance. The absence of his hands leaves a chill on my body. I feel eyes upon us when we step through the ballroom. One woman says: "Did you see them? He should not be dancing with the likes of her. What would the princess say?"

My cheeks warm with a combination of indignation and shame. Who am I dancing with that would upset a princess?

We make our way out onto a deserted balcony which overlooks the impressive gardens below. The breeze is warm, scented with lavender, sweet and floral. Ivy twists around the stone balustrade. I turn to my dancing partner with an unsaid question on my lips. He tears the mask away to answer that question.

Cas?

Chapter Ten

The Failed Escape

"Mae," he says, his voice not as anxious or stilted, but rushed and breathy. "We do not have much time until the princess... I shouldn't have danced like that with you. It's too dangerous."

"But, Cas!" I reach forward and take his hands in mine. "Don't! I want to be with you."

"And I you, but if Ellen, the princess—I hate saying that—if she finds out... You should go. You should leave here," he urges. "She is powerful and she will kill you if she knows. I'm sorry Mae."

Ellen is the princess? But that means they have married. My heart sinks.

He lifts a finger to my face and unhooks the mask. Before I can do anything else, his lips press against mine. It is a gentle kiss, but ignites my senses all the same. I smell that familiar Cas scent, one of sweet and spice. Musk, berries, lemons…

"Come, we must get you to safety. Replace your mask. I know a way out of the castle, and you must take it. You must go, ride away to somewhere safe. I cannot lose you forever, Mae. I cannot."

We rush back into the ballroom and through the throng of people into the corridors. Cas ducks through them, ignoring the stares and whispers. He stops me by a refreshments table and leans towards me as though we are talking.

"Now, don't say anything. There are people watching us. Wait until they become bored and I'll help you leave," he says. "These sweet buns are tasty, aren't they?" He glances over his shoulder. "Right, now."

We slip out of the ballroom and head down the corridor. My shoes click against the stones. I bend down and slip them from my feet. Then I can trot alongside Cas, keeping up with his pace.

"Where are we going?" I ask.

"I'm taking you to the tunnels. Then you need to go to Anta. Ride away from here. It's the only way."

"You're not coming with me?"

He shakes his head. "I can't. I have to think of the realm. My father is ill. If I go now, it will give Lyndon an opportunity to usurp the throne. We both know he will run Aegunlund into the ground. I can't let that happen."

I know he's right, but there's an ache in my stomach.

"Where will I go?"

"To Sasha," he says. "She'll keep you safe in the Borgan camp. I know you're still angry about what happened to your father, but you know she is a good person. She had nothing to do with it."

"I know," I say. "I'll go to Sasha."

Cas comes to a halt, and for the third time since the curse came down on the Red Palace, I find myself at the queen's chambers. He slides the brass rings until the notches line up correctly, then ushers me into the room. There he opens the hidden door in the bathroom by moving another set of the brass rings from the inside. He takes me by the hand and leads me into the secret passageway.

"Will I see you again?" When I say the

words I feel as though I have said them before.

"I don't know," he replies. His face is strained and tense. His jaw is set and juts out, as though he's gritting his teeth. "I'm sorry, Mae."

I pull on his arm. "It's not your fault."

We kiss again, harder this time. His body presses against mine. There's something that feels normal and right, and yet there's another part screaming inside, telling me that I can't stop kissing him, that I must cling to him and never let him go. When he pulls away, I'm left woozy for a moment. I rock back on my heels in a daze. Cas has to pull me on.

The twists and turns of the tunnels are different this time. I try to memorise them as we go, counting the lefts and rights. It all goes past in a blur. Cas's lantern waivers as we hurry, spinning shadows along the walls. It reminds me of a shadow show in the tavern once in Halts-Walden, when the actors made shapes out of their hands. I remember the silhouette of a wolf that frightened me so much I did not sleep for two nights. Father had told me I was too young but I had insisted...

On the left wall, I spot a line of words carved into one of the stones. The words are small, cursive, worn over time. I have to stop and read them, but I don't seem to have any control over my body in this vision. My legs continue to hurry along. I can move my head, but my body won't let me deviate further.

This is it. This is my chance to find out before I am back in my own body and in danger from the Nix. I must make myself. I must learn how to take control of these visions, because this could help me defeat the Nix.

All I can do is hope that the craft will stir within me. If the realm draws on the craft, then that must mean that the Nix's magic is related to mine. If I concentrate on taking control of my body… perhaps…

I think of slowing myself one footstep at a time. I lean back from Cas, trying to ease my hand out of his. My body wills me forward, but I take a deep breath and try to empty my mind. When my hand lets go of Cas, I know I'm almost there. Now I need to slow down my footsteps.

"What's wrong?" Cas says.

"I… I…" Controlling my voice is even harder. I force myself through the barrier. "I need to see something… the words on the wall…"

"What are you talking about? Mae, we have to leave."

"Can't..." I say. "Need to..."

I force my feet back. At first I'm walking backwards because I can't turn around, but as I break down more barriers, I'm able to turn myself in the opposite direction and hurry back along the passageway, searching for those words. Could they be important to my quest to destroy the curse?

"Mae!" Cas calls out. "What are you doing?"

I hear his boots scuff the floor as he rushes back to me.

"There's something here that I need to see," I insist.

"What is it?"

"Here." I point to the words. They say: *En Crypt Saran.*

"It must be some crypt for a person called Saran," Cas says. "Come on we have to go."

"Why would there be a crypt here?"

Cas shrugs. "Who knows what could be in these walls. Some of them are thick enough to hold a body. Perhaps one of the old kings murdered and buried his rival here. I've never really thought about it."

"En Crypt Saran," I say aloud. The words are strange and disjointed.

"Leave it," Cas urges. "Look, there is even a symbol beneath it. Probably a marker for the poor soul stuck in the wall." He rubs away at moss on the stone. It reveals the basic sketch of an eye.

I gasp. "Viewing platform."

"What?" Cas asks.

"Something Beardsley said." I know deep down that this must be the key. There is something to solve here. I lean forward and examine the wall, running my fingers over the bricks. It could be that my imagination is reaching for something that isn't there, but it seems to me that for a rectangle underneath the words, the surface of the stones are smoother. It's a very subtle change, but one that raises my suspicions. Perhaps this is some sort of false wall.

"This is of little importance. Mae, Ellen *knows* about us. It's dangerous for you here."

"What is Ellen going to do?" I ask. I seem to be in full control of myself now. I'm able to talk and walk as I would like.

He shakes his head. "I don't know. But it is dangerous for the king to find out I am with you. He will not stand for it. He and Lyndon would like nothing more than to get rid of me. I swear sometimes they conspire against me at night. There are times when I lay awake, waiting for it to happen. I worry they will go for Mother first. I can't worry about you as well. I... I need you safe, Mae."

"Then I'll go," I say. I am desperate to investigate the wall further, but I am also aware of the fact that I can be hurt, perhaps even killed, in the visions. Not only that, Cas's eyes are wide and pleading, full of bright emotion that I can't resist. I lift a hand and touch his cheek. "I promise I will." And then, in a surge of emotion that comes from my very core, one that almost knocks me off my feet, I find myself saying, "I love you, Cas. I have for longer than I care to admit." Saying the words sends a heat wave up my skin. Being in the vision has made me bold. I forgot myself for a moment. I'm speaking as *me* now, not some puppet in the Nix's vision.

"I love you too," he says with a long breath. He grasps my hand and his eyes bore into mine. My heart pounds. The moment is too fleeting. I want to clutch it and hold on to it. I want time to slow. I want to savour this moment, stretch it out until it reaches infinity twenty times over. More than anything, I want this moment to be real, not part of a sick and twisted game.

"But we have to go," he insists.

I snap out of my trance and nod. We hurry

back along the passage. Cas directs us with ease. I imagine him and his mother practising their escape along these tunnels. The queen was right to ensure her safety in the Red Palace by taking the room by this passageway.

Cas is out of breath and flushed by the time we reach a large, wooden door with a lock combination even more complicated than the last.

"If you go through here, you reach the sewage tunnels out of Cyne. On the border, I'll have a guard waiting with Anta. I'm sorry, Mae. If there was another way. I wish I could come with you."

Unexpected tears prick my eyes. I might now be in control of my body, but my emotions are running high. This is a lot to take in: an affair with Cas? Danger from Ellen? An escape?

"Can I send you a message when I get to Sasha?" I say.

"Send it to my mother. She'll give it to me. Anything directly to me could be dangerous. They're coming for me, Mae. I can feel it."

"Then I should stay and protect you," I reply.

"What can you do? No, I want you in safety."

"I'm stronger than you think."

Cas turns away from me and moves the rings to open the door. It swings open and the smell of the putrid sewage tunnels hits the back of my throat.

"Go," he says.

My eyes mist. I take hold of Cas and kiss him again. This time, I am me, and I have waited for this moment for a long time. I sink into him, and I memorise every moment. I inhale his scent, taste the sweet honey of Cyne sticky buns. I could live my life and only have this moment. Even if it isn't real, I need to remember it. All of it.

When we break, I move towards the sewage tunnel when there is a high-pitched sound like a *zziip* and a *thump*. Something hot hits my back and warm liquid trickles down my hip.

"What…?" I say, stumbling from my woozy head. Cas grasps my wrist, his face filled with horror.

Another *zzip* and a hideous *thump* as another arrow hits my chest. My knees buckle from under me.

A man dressed in gold steps out from the shadows. He grins and his teeth are like wolf's teeth. The king. "I told you I wouldn't miss this time."

As the tunnel fades into darkness, I see Cas's eyes filled with tears.

I wake to searing pain over my body. Both my chest and my back is in agony. The Nix is gone, but blood seeps from both wounds, mingling with the stones on the floor of the castle. There are black spots darting in front of my eyes and I long to close them, until I hear a voice.

"Stay with me, Mae. Don't go to sleep."

"Sasha? What are you doing here?"

There's a swish of red curls. My vision is blurry but I can just make out her pale face staring down at me. "I guess I'm your new protector. Allerton came back to the camp in a right huff. It was dreadfully creepy watching his soul filter back into a lifeless body. No, don't try to move. You've been badly injured. Stay very still."

In my pain, I must have reached out to the Borgans. Only this time, I tore Sasha's soul from her body. Her familiar tone is a comfort to me, but I hate the thought of putting her in danger.

"I can't touch you, Mae, so you need to dress the wounds yourself. It looks like the wound on your chest is bleeding faster than the one on your back. You need to apply pressure."

"This... this isn't the first injury," I say as I try to rip clothing to apply to my chest. "I have a cut on my side, too. And the Nix got my face. It... it's too much. I won't make it."

"Yes you will," she says. "You are the craft-born and you heal fast. Now, press down on the wound on your chest, and think about the earth. Do you remember when we were in the Waerg Woods and the Profeta stabbed you?"

"Yes," I say. "I remember."

"That wound was far worse than these, and it was infected. But you dreamt of the earth. You dreamt of the roots tangled in soil, and it helped to mend you. You must do that now. Dress the cut tightly, and think of those roots."

I follow her instructions, forcing my weak, shaking fingers to pull my makeshift bandage tight.

"It was the king," I mumble. "In a vision. He shot at me because I was with Cas. Cas said he loved me."

Sasha frowns. "Is this another vision from the Nix?"

"I don't know," I say. "I don't know what's real and what's a lie anymore. I'm confused,

Sasha. I don't know what to believe." I almost choke on my own tears. I feel so tired. I'm at breaking point after the Nix's games. The longer this goes on, the less reasoning I see behind it. Now I believe it's little more than an elaborate way to torture and kill me.

"Then believe in yourself. Believe that you are going to survive this and kill that squirmy little shit once and for all," Sasha says. Her mouth tightens into a thin line and her red curls fall over her face. She is dressed in the same hooded cowl all the Borgan's wear.

"I'm glad it's you this time," I say.

"You called me," she replies. "I didn't know I was even a protector, but you called me." She gives a small smile. "I think you missed me."

I laugh, but the pain isn't worth it. My vision begins to cloud and my breaths are ragged.

"No, no, no! Stay with me, Mae." Sasha kneels down by my side, but the corridor is already floating away.

CHAPTER ELEVEN

THE ANCESTORS

The Red Palace isn't silent at all; it's just that we don't listen. If you stay very still, you can hear the sound of thousands of creatures beneath the ground, burrowing and burying. There are just as many roots spreading and growing through the soil. Ancient soil; connected to my ancestors, the Aelfens; walked on by thousands of feet over thousands of years; steeped in history, enriched by the bodies of our dead. I feel the magic as I feel my own extremities. The soil is my blood. My life force. It is as though there is no stone between us. No castle basement. The barrier has lifted. I have become one with the mud, and its nutrients flow through me like the magic.

Nature exists in all things, and therefore so does the craft.

Allerton told me that once. He was right. I *feel* the magic in the soil, and I am at one with it. We've become bound together in a great tangle of limbs and roots.

As I am barely conscious I hear Sasha singing the same song she sang through the Waerg Woods, about a girl with a broken heart who begged for the tree to pull her down into the ground. I understand that now. I understand how it is possible to join the soil — to long for it.

As I lay dying, my mind drifts from reality to insanity. My thoughts are fractured, with parts of the Nix's riddles coming to me in segments:

I devour hearts.
You cannot touch me, but I make you cold,
Who am I?
Trailing silk, I glide
I'm always wrong and so are you.
Who am I?

First comes the mental torture, and now the physical injuries. Has the Nix gone too far? Has it killed me at last?

There's a special kind of peace spreading from my toes, and I suspect that it is the magic trying to soothe away the pain.

But it's when I see her that I know I *am* going insane.

At first, I think it is another Nymph come to hurt me. She is iridescent in her loveliness, and glows like the Glowbugs in the Waerg Woods. But as she approaches, I see her dark skin and hair black as night. I see the strange blue eyes, and her full lips.

She is naked and should be ashamed of her exposed body. But somehow she is not. She seems neither boastful, nor bashful. She holds her head up high, her shoulders are thrown back, and yet her eyes are soft, misted with dew. She looks at me in the same way the queen looks at Cas, like a proud mother, with her mouth turned into a sad smile. Wet eyes and glowing skin and gentle features. She is beautiful.

She crouches next to me and lays a warm hand on my cool forehead.

"Who are you?" I ask.

Close up, I see even more of her beauty. Her eyes are oval and framed by curled lashes. The symmetry of her face is so striking that you feel yourself pulled in by her presence.

"I am Avery, little one."

"What do you want with me?"

"I want you to live, of course. You seem to be giving up, and I can't have that at all."

"Why is the Nix trying to kill me?"

"Why, I don't believe it is, dear one. But its intentions are not pure at all, and I am very sorry for everything it is putting you through." She glances at my wound and raises an eyebrow. "Such a cruel way to try and obtain what it wants from you." The corner of her mouth lifts in amusement. She raises her hand from my forehead.

"I need to help Cas," I whisper. "And I must find Anta."

"Yes, you will need to be alive to help your prince." She hesitates and a small frown plays on her lips. "I am sorry for what you will endure. It is almost too much for a little one like you. Never stray from your path and remain as strong as the oldest tree in the Waerg Woods. There will come a time in the future when you have a difficult decision to make, dear Mae. You must go with your heart when it comes. Always trust your heart, and always trust the magic within you."

She stands straight and tall and backs away. As she leaves, a thread of heat works its way through my fingers. I can feel the knitting of my chest as my wounds begin to heal.

She steps back, singing softly as she goes:

Over yellow sands,
Our girl will weep,
Great river run,
Calm the drought.

Under yellow sands,
Our girl will cry,
Streams flow free,
An ache subsides,

Win for us,
Our girl will try.
Strong of heart,
Of will, of mind.

We wait, we wait.
We're free, we're free!
But never she.
Never she.

"Mae? Mae?"

As I begin to wake, I am vaguely aware of Sasha leaning over me. She seems so real that I almost ask her to help me up.

"I have work to do," I say, attempting to sit and experiencing another searing bout of pain explode in my chest.

"Oh no you don't," she says. You need to sleep. I wish I could help tend to your injuries but I can't touch you." She lowers her voice. "Mae, I was frightened for you."

"I'm fine," I say. "Avery helped me."

"Avery? Who?" Sasha replies. "Never mind. The Nix is not here. You must sleep and help the wound heal. Keep using your craft, Mae. Let it heal you."

Now I know why the craft-born needs the Borgans. Without Sasha I would be drifting and alone. I would be frightened and weak, like a small child. Her presence gives me strength.

Back in Halts-Walden, I had always thought that I didn't like the company of others. Perhaps I told myself that to make myself feel better when the other villagers kept their distance. It simply isn't true. In fact, it is the opposite. I think I have always been afraid to be alone. That is why Father's death left such a large hole in my life and why Casimir's presence brought me such comfort.

The problem is—I am not used to being around anyone except Father. I don't know how to be someone's friend. I didn't think I even knew how to love anyone except him. At least, not at first.

Love.

The word sits heavy on my heart. Did I ever tell Father how much I love him? Did he die without knowing?

It wasn't Cas's vision version of me who told him she loved him, it was me. It came from me, and there was part of me that wasn't even sure if I did. After those long weeks in the Waerg Woods, the nights around the fire, and the ways in which we rescued each other. It has been a slow progression that has built with intensity.

How long has he been sleeping in the basement of the palace? How long have we been apart?

Those moments in his vision have left another hole, one which burns away like an ember that refuses to die. If there is even one iota of truth in Cas's vision...

Oh, the Nix is clever. It uses every trick it can to play with my mind. How long will it be before it uses the death of my Father, too? I clench my fists as I lay on the stone floor, waiting for my wounds to heal. I drift in and out of consciousness, listening to Sasha's melodic hums.

I want sleep, now. I want a dreamless sleep where I am alone. There I can mend.

I'm not sure how many more cruel tricks I can stand from the Nix. I don't know who to believe, or what is real. How can I be hurt in some visions and not in others? It must be when I am me. When I am in someone else, or when I am a bystander, I come away unscathed. It is the Nix's way of punishing me for trying to take control.

Perhaps that means I am close to defeating it. If the Nix needs to weaken me in every vision, it means that I am doing something that must be quelled. Avery mentioned the hardships I endure. What if this is all a test?

I try to sort through what I have discovered from the visions so far.

Beardsley is afraid of something he created for the king.

Trailing silk, I glide, spin patterns to catch you, suck you dry.

The spider. I shudder at the thought.

Ellen is afraid of her father, and of her love for a girl.

I am there in the faint of heart,
But I rarely visit the bold.

Fear. The Nix repeated this riddle twice. It was warning me of the fears.

Both Cas and the queen are afraid of Lyndon.

I am in you.

Evil. Evil is in all of us, but there is more in Lyndon than anyone else I have met. Even the king.

Cas is afraid... for me? Or that he loves me? I can't work out Cas's fears. Some of the visions show his perspective of my own memories. No, not my memories, the memories that the Nix has chosen to show me. They could be twisted memories for all I know, teasing me of what might have been but what could never happen because Cas will never love me. He isn't here to ask.

Whatever you see, he will never love you. It will not be because of the craft-born imposter, it will be because you lied to him.

You will break your heart in two.
I'm always wrong and so are you.

My emotions are too tangled with this vision. I cannot think clearly. For the time being I must disregard my last vision with Cas and concentrate on the facts.

Other things I have learned:

The king has a journal with the combinations of many of the locks in the castle.

There is some sort of code in the tunnels. *En Crypt Saran.* I don't believe it to be a crypt at all.

The king is in debt to the Haedalands.

The king has paid for weapons to be forged.

The payment to blacksmiths and the debts in the Haedalands could at least mean unrest. There's a chance that the king is stockpiling weapons as a precaution. But why put the realm in yet more debt for the sake of extra weaponry? When I read Father's books on the old wars, they almost always began when one region wanted something from the other. They usually made up excuses, like the execution of a family member, or the dissolution of a marriage, but really one king wanted to steal from another king. I saw a lot of greed in those books, and I already know the king is greedy.

But as I consider the king's motives, there is an itchy feeling inside that tells me there is more to all this. Why would the Nix care about a war? Even though part of me has begun to believe that this is all a sadistic ruse to torture and kill me, I know deep down that it doesn't make sense to go to such efforts. There has to be more to it.

Allerton was right. The key to all this is learning to use my powers. If I can channel the craft, I can not only fight the Nix, but grow strong enough to control the visions. If I can control them, I can figure out what it is the Nix wants. There is too much manipulation within these visions. I have to take some of the control.

Sasha's humming soothes my mind as I relax. I can do nothing while I am injured. It's time to let the craft mend me, and as I meditate on my powers, I feel them blossom inside. It's like the opening of a flower in spring. I'm reminded of the sunflowers that grow in Halts-Walden. Even though our cabin overlooked the dark woods, the sunflowers grew strong and tall. Many of the wives in the village were jealous of our garden. Little did they know that it has always been my connection with nature that has allowed them to flourish.

I must concentrate on the knitting of my flesh. I take deep breaths and imagine myself to be tiny enough to hide in droplets of my blood. The thought of blood and torn flesh is hideous, and yet it gives me some comfort to think of these things as they multiply and mend. I become whole again.

"Mae, how are you doing?"

"How long have I been sleeping?" I ask.

"A few hours... actually, that's a lie. Almost a day."

I bolt upright and feel a twinge in my chest. "A *day*? Why didn't you wake me?"

I check on my wounds with Sasha's supervision. They are healing well. Together we move through the castle back to the kitchen where I can eat and regain strength. I have no fear of the Nix now. It did not kill me when it had the chance. Instead, it left me to heal. I do not believe that the Nix wants me dead. I am a tool in its game, essential for as long as it needs me.

"This soul-rip is odd," Sasha says. "I can't touch, or feel. It's like I'm not human anymore."

"A ghost," I reply, my mouth filled with apple.

"Don't say that," she says. There's a warning in her eyes, a glassiness. "It's not right."

"I'm sorry," I say. "I didn't mean... it doesn't mean you're dead."

"I know. It's just frightening to know my

body is out there. It feels vulnerable somehow, like I'm unable to protect it. And I'm hardly able to protect you, too. I can't help tend to your wounds, or fight the Nix. I can't do anything."

"Yes you can. You can use your mind. Your presence helps me," I say. "I've missed you."

Sasha feigns shock. "A kind word from Mae Waylander? Is the sky now green and the grass blue?"

I can't help it, I laugh, but then I think of all that has happened and the laugh fizzles out. "There's been so much going on since I got to the Red Palace. First I had to work with Ellen to trick the king. Then I decided to leave Ellen and Cas. Then I've been sent into these visions where the worst fears of some of the court members come alive. I've seen... terrible things. It's all happened in a blur. I can't... I can't slow it down. I..."

Sasha bows her head. "I'm sorry, Mae."

I take another bite of my apple and try to push it all aside. "It's fine. I can deal with it."

"Why did you send Allerton away?" Sasha asks.

I shrug my shoulders and stare down at my apple, almost chewed to the core. "I believe that Allerton wanted to protect me. I think I was beginning to trust him, and I know his knowledge was helping me. He has a lot of wisdom." I shake my head and let out a sigh. "But he isn't a good man, I don't think."

Sasha regards me with a blank expression. She blinks twice and maintains her gaze. It's non-judgemental and somehow puts me at ease.

"I haven't fully forgiven him but I am working on it. That wasn't the reason, though. When we met him in the Borgans tent, he never showed a good side to him. He was always giggling and laughing at things that weren't funny. He had Ellen trapped in a cage and regarded her with disdain. He isn't a good person, Sasha, I can feel it. You *are* a good person. You're the one I want protecting me. Not him."

Sasha leans towards me. "I wish I could hold your hands and pledge my allegiance—"

"No," I say. "I'm not royal. I'm not a queen. I don't want you to pledge yourself to me. You're my friend. That's all I ever want from you." Inexplicable tears fill my eyes. I'm unsure as to whether they are tears of joy or tears of pain. Perhaps both; joy that Sasha and I are together, and pain that neither Cas, Father, or Anta are here.

Sasha swallows thickly and turns away. "I will be the best friend you've ever had. You can count on that." Then she turns to me with a wicked grin. "And I forgive you for choking me."

I let out a hollow laugh. "I'm sorry for that. I was full of anger after my father died."

"And you're not now?"

"It seems pointless. It created a barrier between me and my feelings. I don't want to let that happen again."

"A barrier between yourself and your feelings is a barrier between yourself and happiness," Sasha says.

I'd never thought about it like that before, but of course she is right. How could I ever let someone love me, or even be happy, if I couldn't feel it for myself?

After a long pause, Sasha clears her throat. "I am here to help you. So far I know you are stuck in the Red Palace and that you have been hurt by the Nix. You mentioned that you have been in the worst fears of *other* people. That is something I have never heard of before. We need to work out how to stop all this. Tell me everything you know."

I don't hold back on any detail and Sasha sits patiently as I recall the last couple of days.

It has all been such a blur that I find myself going back and adding in details as I remember them.

"So you have the king's personal journal?" she asks.

"Yes," I say. "It has all the lock combinations—"

"And what about his private thoughts? Have you read them? Have you read the journal at all?"

I pull the small book from my pocket. I haven't read any of it. "I've been too busy with the Nix."

"Well read it, Mae. Everything seems to go back to the king when you think about it," she says. "The queen has a secret passageway to get away from him. The designer of the castle is afraid of him. His youngest son wants to *be* him. There's some sort of secret laboratory somewhere. He owes money to rich people in the Haedalands, and he has already commissioned weapons for some sort of war. You need to read that book if you're to outwit whatever the Nix wants."

I crack the well-worn spine and open the book to the first page.

I am in despair.

CHAPTER TWELVE

THE KING'S JOURNAL

I am in despair. I need Beardsley to end this. If what they tell me is true, there is nothing else I can do about it. The end will come and I will be powerless.

I am the King, born to a bloodline chosen by the Gods. I will not accept my fate. I will not sit idly by and let this happen to me. I have not worked at keeping my crown against the usurpers who wish to take it away from me only to have it prised from my cold fingers in such a humiliating fashion. This turn of events is unacceptable to me.

Beardsley tells me that there is a solution, but it is somewhat of a legend. I believe it exists, and I believe it is in Aegunlund. I just don't know where. I will make sure that Beardsley uses his damn brain to acquire it for me. There has to be a way. He says that it is tied to the magic of the realm. Why does everything have to come back to the damn craft-

born? It adds insult to injury that it is always a useless girl given the power. The king should have the power.

Never mind, it will be of no concern in the end. I will uncover this secret even if I have to drain the craft-born of the last drop of blood in her body.

It will be mine, and with it I will become a God.

"What does all this mean?" I say out loud.

Sasha shakes her head. "It sounds like the king is afraid of losing the throne."

"He wants to drain my blood in order to keep the crown?" I say with a shake of my head. "I don't think so! The man is a maniac."

We carry on reading, but the journals are the ramblings of either a drunk or a deranged man. Anyone who thinks they will become a God can't be in his right mind. But then I think of Allerton's stories about the Gods I had always thought created us, not the other way around, and wonder if more is possible than I had ever thought before.

"Do you think it could be the Nix? He could be afraid of the Nix?" I say.

"It's possible," Sasha replies.

It's black, all black. I see nothing, only the ever stretching dark. It lies before me, waiting, waiting.

And inside grows the evil. It is consuming me as I breathe.

Beardsley, that useless old lump. He has not come up with a way to find it without the magic, and there is not a craft-born to be found. I will make that magical bitch marry my son if it is the last thing I do.

No, no, not the last. Never the last.

Find it. He must find it.

I shake my head. "None of this makes sense. He could be looking for anything." I slam the book closed. "It's probably a diamond so he can pay off those he owes in the Haedalands. Or he's looking for a way to finance his stupid war." When I think of the king it makes my blood boil. It should be Cas on the throne, not this rambling mad man.

And inside grows the evil.

It *sounds* like an insane thing to say, and yet there is truth there too. He *is* evil through and through. It shows that he has some awareness at least; unless he is talking about something else, like his favourite son, Lyndon.

"There's more to all this," Sasha says. "The king isn't just crazy. He wouldn't be able to function if he was. He wouldn't be able to rule. There are plenty of power hungry people who would gladly take the throne if they had the chance. He's managed to maintain his position of power despite being verging on destitute. That takes cunning and manipulation and fear. Insanity is not as frightening as ruthlessness. Trust me, if he really is as crazy as that journal suggests, he wouldn't still be king. "

I think for a moment. The answer lies in all of this somewhere, and I know that I only need to put the pieces together, but everything is going off in different directions and I find the pressure of it all overwhelming.

"We need to go back to the tunnels," I say. "There was some sort of code written on one of the stones and I think it might be useful. *En Crypt Saran.* Cas said he thought it was a crypt, a dead foe buried in the walls of the secret passageway, but I think that's hogwash. I think it is a clue. I had a feeling in my stomach that it was important."

"Cas was there with you?" she asks.

"A vision version of him. An imposter made up by the Nix," I say.

Sasha regards me with that annoying assessing look she often gives me. "Mae, in these visions, is Cas... romantic with you?"

I squirm away from her. "I don't know what you mean."

"Yes you do, and I will take that as a yes."

"I know what you're going to say, so don't bother saying it. The Nix is playing a game with me. The Cas in the visions is not really him and I shouldn't believe a word of it."

"In fact, no, that isn't what I was going to say at all," Sasha replies. "The Nix feeds on fear, but it needs an *actual* fear to feed from. It needs something that is true. That's why, when it stalks its prey, it learns everything it can about its prey. When the Nix caught my mother in the Waerg Woods, I believe it used all that knowledge to frighten her to death. Without the truth, the vision would not scare us."

"But the Nix is targeting me, not Cas."

"Is it?" she replies. "You said that you have been in Ellen's greatest fear, and Beardsley and the queen, do they sound like they are about you?"

"No, I suppose not. I didn't even feature in some of them. I was inside the person. Like a passenger."

"Exactly. Perhaps the Nix is using a valid fear from Cas to torment you with. Maybe Cas really does have feelings for you," she suggests.

"And *that* is his greatest fear?"

"Think about it. He is a young boy engaged to a girl he doesn't know. He's forced into this marriage, Mae. Don't you think that would mess with his head? He has to *believe* he loves her because he has no choice. And all this time he has spent with you, knowing you, being in life threatening situations, all of that must have confused him further. To Cas, letting down his people, his king and his mother is probably his greatest fear. Being in love with you could be his greatest fear."

It is as though someone has shone a bright light in my eyes. I see nothing. I feel numb.

"I don't... I don't believe it," I whisper, even though every part of my body *wants* to believe it.

"Oh stop being a nincompoop." Sasha waves a dismissive hand in front of her face. "Anyway, we have far more important things to worry about than *boys*."

"You brought it up," I remind her.

"Yes, good point. I might try not to do that from now on. Boys are so very boring."

I climb to my feet and wince at the sharp twang in my chest. Even with the fast heeling my injuries still smart. We make our way back to the secret tunnel where this all began. I've been at this very spot many times now. It makes me wonder if the queen had her suspicions regarding the curse. I now believe she brought me to this very room on purpose. But why would she bring me and not Ellen? Surely the craft-born—in her eyes—would have been a better choice.

I now have the combinations memorised. The effort is uncomfortable with my injuries, but I push through the pain. We are in the tunnels in no time and I am eager to find secrets I have never seen before, not even after exploring the castle before the curse fell. I used to follow the royal members as they moved around the palace, fascinated by the twists and turns of the long corridors. I have a reputation for remaining unseen in Halts-Walden, it wasn't hard to spy on many members of the court.

But I never followed the king. I didn't want to be anywhere near him after what he did to me in the Waerg Woods. Perhaps that was a mistake. Then again, how was I to know that the curse and its responsibilities would fall on my shoulders? One thing I never seem to understand is that all my actions seem to be training for something worse. Whenever I think I have overcome a problem, I step around a corner and into something worse.

"I think it was around this bend and down those steps," I say to Sasha as we press on.

She runs her fingers through her hair and purses her lips. "It's dark down here. I don't like small spaces, not even when I am little more than a soul."

"You can walk through walls you know," I say, holding the lantern higher to light our way.

She shudders. "No thank you. Especially not if there are dead bodies in the wall."

I laugh. "Come on, just a little further. Oh, here it is."

I move the lantern closer to the writing on the wall. Those three words again:

En Crypt Saran.

"Blessed Celine, how creepy. Are you sure it isn't a crypt? It certainly sounds like it. And, no, I will not be walking into the wall to find this 'Saran' person," Sasha says.

"Saran sounds a little like a Borgan name," I observe.

"There are no Sarans in the camp as far as I'm aware. I don't think I've ever heard such a name before."

"Nor I. In fact, I don't think it's a name at all." I brush away the moss from beneath the words to reveal the eye symbol. "Beardsley mentioned a viewing area for the secrets in the castle. I think Beardsley would mark such a place, and an eye would be perfect, don't you think?"

"Yes, actually. It does make sense."

"And look at the stone here. It's smoother, I can feel it. The colour is slightly off. All around this area, the stones have darkened over time. This portion is lighter, as though a picture has hung here or it has been cleaned."

"But to be fair," Sasha says. "There *could* have been a picture hung here, and the caption could have related to the picture."

"True. But listen to the words: *En Crypt.* Encrypt. It's like it's telling me to solve the puzzle."

"But how could you solve *Saran.* We've already established that it isn't a name, and it's certainly not a word I know. Maybe it's in another language, Jakani or, Gods forbid, Ibena."

I shudder at the mention of the Ibenas. The memory of them trying to sacrifice me to their Gods is still fresh in my mind. "No, I don't think so. When Father taught me to read we used to read history books about the monarchs of Aegunlund. During the war between the Jakanis and the Southern Archipelagos, King Frederick used to send letters written in code. He used the alphabet and assigned each letter a number."

"Well, I don't see any numbers here," Sasha replies.

"No, I suppose not. I don't really know anything else about encryptions. You have to have the code in order to crack it."

"Well, yes, Mae." Sasha rolls her eyes at me. "Unless it's just a jumble of letters. Perhaps if we reorder them—"

"—we'll uncover the clue," I finish. We turn to each other. Sasha is grinning and I am filled with renewed energy.

"Snap," Sasha begins.

"Prance," I add.

"Rant."

"Cane. Pry?"

"Carry. Ants. Pen?"

"Trans... Tran..."

"Transparen... wait, no."

And then we say together. "Transparency!"

We turn to the words on the wall expectantly, but nothing happens.

"What did we do wrong?" I say.

"I don't think it's a magic word," Sasha replies. "Didn't you say it was an inventor who created this castle?"

"Yes."

"I don't think an inventor could use enough craft to create a spell like that. You must have to use the word somehow."

"You mean write it?" I say.

"It could work."

I lift my finger and carefully trace the word along the stone. As I silently spell it in my mind I thank my father for forcing me to read as a child. Many of the peasants never bothered to learn when they were children, and I had always hated book learning. Now it is has become invaluable to me, and the thought of never sitting down with my father and a book, it leaves an ache in my heart.

I shake my head as I finish the last letter. "No. It hasn't opened."

"There must be something in here," Sasha says. "A place to write the word, or move the letters."

We search the wall, but there is nothing. I press my hand against every inch, expecting something to move. But there is nothing. I let out a sigh and place the lantern on a sconce.

My eyes are drawn to the joist holding the lantern. Could it be so simple? I've heard of bookcases containing trick books, and candle holders that turn. I reach up and twist the joist left. It doesn't budge. Right, it turns.

Sasha gasps as there is a scrape of stone against stone. Above the lettering, a small oblong box appears. Inside the box are twelve letters, each corresponding with *En Crypt Saran*. When I touch them, I find that they slide along the edges of the box, meaning I can rearrange them.

T R A N S P A R E N C Y

I hold my breath. In the first instant, nothing moves. There is no sound. My heart sinks. And then, like smoke filtering from the air, the stone dissipates into glass.

"It was an illusion," Sasha says with a sigh.

"Or coloured glass," I point out.

She shakes her head. "An illusion, it had to be. That means the craft was involved. No one has looked through this window since the last craft-born died."

Mentioning the craft brings weight down on my shoulders. This is a monumental moment. We have beaten the code, and now we will discover the greatest secret in the Red Palace.

Sasha leans forward. "Wow, how far down

does this thing go?"

The scene from the window takes my breath away. Right in the centre of the castle, somewhere between the first and second floor, is a cylindrical room that tunnels down, down into the bowels of the palace. Around the wall of the room is a set of stairs spiralling into the darkness below. And in the centre grows a tall, metal structure, reaching up almost to the window, brass coloured and covered in strange levers and arms. I recognise it at once as a Beardsley invention.

The spiral staircase has intermittent platforms at different levels. Each platform juts out towards the metal structure. They could be areas used to maintain the equipment. Places to stand and work.

"Look, this part of the glass is magnified." Sasha points to a thicker portion at the bottom of the window. "You can see all the way down."

I move closer to the window and gaze through the magnified portion. I've never known glass like this before. Sometimes a hunter would stay in the Fallen Oak in Halts-Walden with fancy spectacles that could see further than the eye. I never got the chance to look through them so I can't say if Beardsley's is better or worse, but the effect is so startling that I can make out even the smallest details down at the bottom of the room.

It appears that the metal structure sits atop a furnace, which is unused for the moment. Around the room is a circular bench covered in beakers and glasses. There are what seem to be tiny pieces of glass covering the surface of the bench, sparkling bright.

"It looks like a laboratory," I say. "But the king already has a laboratory in the West Wing of the castle. Why would he want another?"

"To perform secret experiments I bet," Sasha replies.

I step back away from the glass. The metal structure is curious, I can't imagine what it does or how it works. I notice a pipe running along the edge of the spiral staircase. When I examine the magnified portion once more, it seems as though the mouth of the pipe opens out onto the bench around the room. Whatever this structure makes, it comes out at the bottom.

"Do you know how far this room goes down? Is it lower than the cellar?" Sasha asks.

"I think it must be. I think it might go as far as the crypts." I shudder slightly as I say the word. I've never ventured into the crypts below the castle because I've never wanted to.

"I guess there's only one way to find out," Sasha says.

The tunnels are a maze between the regular rooms of the castle, and, without the familiar tapestries and ornaments to follow, it's easy to lose your bearings. After taking more than one wrong turn, we decide to head back to the queen's room and work our way down to the crypts from there. As we walk, I find my thoughts drifting to my last vision with Cas. I used to wonder what it would be like to kiss Cas when we were travelling through the Waerg Woods. Now I know.

I can still taste him.

Like the sweet pastries in Halts-Walden.

But it wasn't real.

I miss his presence. I miss waking to the sunrise, and seeing him sat by the fire keeping watch, his chin on his fist and his eyes hooded over. More than anything, I miss his counsel. It took me too long to warm up to him, but once I did, I enjoyed talking to him. We would share our problems. He didn't always know what to do, but he always comforted me.

What we shared in the Waerg Woods can never be replicated. I will never go through that experience with anyone else. No one else will ever know. Not even Sasha.

I pull a deep breath in through my nose and attempt to quell the stirring of emotions deep beneath the surface.

"You should practice fire as we walk," Sasha says. "If it comes down to a fight —"

"I know, I know. It's the Nix's greatest fear."

"What's blocking you?" she asks.

I rub my clammy palms against my clothes. "It's hard to describe how I feel. Worn out, is the easiest way to say it. I'm worn out with the idea of being angry. I don't want to tap into that emotion anymore. It doesn't feel safe or right, somehow."

"Well, of all our emotions, anger is probably the most dangerous. It is a destructive and unpleasant, I suppose. I can certainly understand why you might think of it like that. Why don't you try praying to Endwyn? Fire doesn't always have to be destructive. It can be creative too. It's a fuel. It's energy. You just need to learn how to redirect that energy in a positive way." She shrugs, as though it's the easiest thing in the world.

I let out a laugh. "I've never really prayed

before, but I suppose it can't hurt."

"Think of it as meditation, or deep focus. Think strongly of fire, of the God of fire, and the creative aspect of it."

I follow Sasha's direction, and all through the castle, as we cross the ballroom, tread the stone slabs of the basement, pass Beardsley's office where Cas sleeps, I focus of Endwyn. I've never seen an effigy. I don't know what He or It or even She looks like, I picture a huge bonfire, stretching up to the sky. But every time, that bonfire becomes the funeral pyre for my father, and every time it is as though the God of fire is laughing down at me.

Finally, we come to a narrow passageway. On the lintel read the words:

Silence for the lost.

As I step beneath the stone passageway a chill creeps down my spine.

CHAPTER THIRTEEN

THE SILENT KINGS

We walk into the dark. I light a torch on the wall and carry it aloft as we move down the steep, stone steps towards the crypt. I cringe each time my footsteps echo through the hall. *Silence for the lost.* Lost. It implies they might come back one day, that we have simply misplaced them.

"This feels like a dangerous place for a soul to be," Sasha says. "Do you think I'll end up trapped in a sarcophagus or something?"

"I hope not," I reply. "This is why we burn our dead in Halts-Walden. The thought of my body ending up down here in the dark depths…"

Sasha nods. "I know what you mean."

Down and down we go. I'm shaking so badly I have to grasp the torch with both my hands to steady it. Up ahead I see the door to the crypt. It is another brass door with the same loops designed by Beardsley. I hang the torch on a sconce as I pull the king's journal and flip to the back pages. It takes some effort to move the rings, but eventually I hear the *click* of the lock and the door swings open with a creak. We both stand there, neither wanting to move forward. I swallow, my mouth and throat dry.

Retrieving the torch from the sconce, I move forward into the crypt. It's a long room, with the walls covered in strange box-like shelves containing marble coffins. I find it an odd way to store the dead, as though they have been neatly folded away into drawers.

At small alcoves between these shelves there are candles fitted to the walls. As we pass each of them, I light the candle, filling the room with a little bit of light with each step. But as the flames dance, it creates more shadows, and more movement, which in turn sends shivers down my spine.

In the distance there is the scuttling sound of a rat—at least I hope it is a rat—moving through the room.

"This laboratory had better be worth it," Sasha says.

"If we can figure out how to kill the Nix, it will be," I add.

After lighting three more candles, the shelves come to an end, and instead we see lines of sarcophagi positioned on the ground by the walls. These coffins are chiselled from marble, higher than our waists, and on top of each one is a depiction of the inhabitant at rest, with their arms softly crossed over, holding their favourite weapon, or, for the women, clutching their favourite jewellery.

"Here lies Catherine Xeniathus, wife of Andrei the Second, Queen, Mother, Wife, Sister. May Celine grant her eternal flight," I read from one of the marble coffins. "I read about her in one of Father's books. She had her own brother hanged for treason because she thought him a threat to the throne. Andrei the Second was an idiot, apparently. She did most of the ruling." Her features are captured in the marble; strong, high cheekbones and a large nose. I look for a resemblance to Cas—she is his ancestor after all—but I find none.

"These people are prominent members of the royal families of old," Sasha says. There is a trace of excitement in her voice as the words rush out, breathy and fast. "There may be kings here, too."

We walk a little further along the still room. At the end of the room is a dead end, blocked off by the last wall. "Ethelbert and his wife. They married for love and then he went insane and cut off his wife's finger with a dagger."

Sasha raises her eyebrows at me. "Do you know everything about the royal family?"

"No," I say, "Only as much as I learned from these five books on history that Father had. He traded them for wood once and taught me to read. He said I needed to better myself. We read those same five books over and over again. Look, Gregor the First." I gaze down upon Gregor's face. "He was ugly. And fat. Look at the size of him!"

Sasha giggles. "Mae, you can't."

"You're right, this is serious," I reply. Seeing the coffins of the royals has sent me giddy, in a strange, morbid way. "He is fat, though. Imagine being married to that lump. He beat every one of his five wives, and they all died in suspicious circumstances. This is for all the women you tortured, you great horrible old bastard." In a moment of madness I kick the edge of the coffin, tripping myself and falling backwards, landing on the hilt of the dead man's sword. To my surprise, the sword depresses into the coffin and there is a scraping sound, followed by heat at my ankles.

"Mae, watch out!" Sasha cries.

A jet of flames burst from underneath the sarcophagus. I leap over them, but the cuff of my trousers is on fire. I let out a scream and beat at my clothes until the fire goes out.

"What in the Gods…" I mutter.

Sasha comes over to me. "The burn is minimal. You should be fine. It will be uncomfortable for a while."

"Uncomfortable," I repeat. "A straw mattress is uncomfortable, this is something else. Where in the name of Celine did those flames come from?"

Sasha kneels down on the stone floor. "There's some sort of pipe attached to the bottom of the coffin. When you leant on the sword it seemed to trigger the flames. There must be a mechanism inside that triggered the reaction. Do you think this could be a clue? I mean, we know that the laboratory is down here somewhere, but there isn't a visible door. It has to be hidden."

"And the trigger to opening the door has been disguised as part of the tombs," I say.

"Yes, that makes sense. It must be booby trapped."

"Be very careful, Mae. We don't know what else is down here."

I nod, and make my way around the room, lifting my torch into each nook and cranny, being especially careful not to touch anything, especially not the marble coffins. The pipe and the fire has Beardsley written all over it. What else has he modified in the palace? Spikes coming out of the floor? Moving walls? Whatever he has done, he has hidden it well. There are no obvious changes in stone patterns or bricks. The walls are normal. But there is one thing that catches my eye. Above the sarcophagi there are words chiselled into the wall. At first I thought it had been an epitaph, but now I realise it is the only poem written on the wall instead of the actual coffins.

I read it aloud.

Here lie leaders of men,
Kings of the Realm,
They gave their lives to protect,
To serve,
To honour.

Watch over them, Gods,

Celine of air,
Ren of water,
Endwyn of fire,
Fenn of soil.

May the light guide you through.

"There's nothing unusual about that," Sasha notes. "It's a tribute to the kings."

"But the fire came from Gregor's tomb. Fire is in the poem."

"Yes, but it was a trap. I don't see how they could create a weapon out of air, water or soil," she replies.

"I don't know, Beardsley is very inventive. I'm sure he would find a way." I read the poem again in my mind, searching for clues. Beardsley seems to like putting a fail-safe in his creations, a hint in case he or whoever else needs the code forgets it. "The Gods are in a particular order. I think we need to press on the sarcophagi in the order of the Gods."

"But how do we know which king relates to which God? I would never have picked Gregor as relating to fire."

"No, it makes sense. There was a fire in Cyne during his reign. It destroyed most of the market square and hundreds died. *That's* why he's fire. See, the king, or any future king, will know the history of his ancestors. He will be able to figure out the clues on the walls," I say.

"You wouldn't think anything of it unless you were looking for it," Sasha says. "And it's disrespectful to kick the coffins of the dead." She shoots me a narrow-eyed look. "Which means it's unlikely anyone would accidentally come across the room. Who would come down here anyway? Except for members of the Royal family."

"We need to figure out which king goes with which God, and then activate the levers. Gregor is fire, and he comes third. We need air first. Do you remember any abnormal storms? High winds that made history?"

"History lessons aren't much of a high priority in the Borgan camp. We're too busy hunting for food and staying alive."

I ignore Sasha and think. "Ethelbert sent ships towards the Southern Archipelagos once. High winds caused a huge tidal wave to wipe out the entire fleet. But that could be water as well as air. Or I think there may have been tales of a hurricane coming from the Sverne mountains and destroying villages in the North when Alfred the Third ruled."

"Choose carefully," Sasha warns.

I stand between the two coffins in thought. "It has to be Alfred."

"Are you sure? You said it was rumours."

"Yes. That's the beauty of it. I think the king would like that people outside his family would be unsure of the real truth. I think he would choose Alfred." With my palms sweating, I move over to the coffin. I swallow and move my hand gently towards the marble.

"Get ready to run," Sasha calls.

My muscles are wound tight. My nerves are jangling. My hand hovers over the hilt of the marble sword resting on the chest of the chiselled statue. Alfred died young, and his effigy is thin, delicate almost. I lower my hand until there is barely a hair's breadth between my skin and the cold surface of the coffin. The burn on my ankle is sore enough to send me a warning, but I must brave myself against the nerves, and believe in myself, just like Avery told me to. I take a deep breath and press down, ready to dart back if anything comes towards me.

The marble grinds together as the hilt depresses. I brace myself for the unexpected, perhaps an axe swinging above my head, or pressurised air jetted towards me, but instead there is silence, and the brightening of light behind me.

"Mae, look!"

I move back from Alfred's coffin and turn to face Sasha. She grins and points down to the ground beneath her feet. Around the stone flag glows a beam of light, highlighting the cracks between the stones.

"Let the light guide you," she says. "It worked! You chose correctly."

As I exhale through my teeth I'm momentarily stunned. I hadn't, until that moment, thought it would actually work.

"You need water next," Sasha says. "Didn't you say Ethelbert lost a fleet of ships?"

"Yes, but I'm not sure if it's in the same theme. The others were disasters that happened in and around Cyne. This was part of military action."

"It was still a natural disaster though," she points out. "It was a tidal wave."

"But there was also a great flood. It came in off the Sea of Solitude and flooded inland as far as Cyne. Thousands died, but I don't remember the king." I walk up and down between the sarcophagi. "It wasn't Gregor, Ethelbert or Alfred the Third. It might have been Andrei or maybe... yes, maybe it was Alfred the Second. No, I think that's right."

"Are you sure?" Sasha says.

"I think I remember now. Alfred the Second's son was killed because he was visiting whores near the coast."

"Where in all of Aegunlund did your father acquire these history books?"

"Oh, it didn't say that. It said he 'frequented a tavern for gambling and sport' but I'm not stupid." I stride over to the coffin and lift my hand to depress the hilt of the sword. Beads of sweat break on my forehead, and I imagine myself lost in a tidal wave, drowned beneath the palace. No, I must believe. I press down on the hilt with less hesitation than before. This must be correct.

The glow behind me indicates that I am. I turn to see a grinning Sasha.

"And now, Gregor," she says.

"Yes," I reply, but I take a moment to check through the facts in my mind. I have to be certain.

The third stone lights up when I press the hilt. There is now only one stone between us and the far wall. If I guess the next king correctly, we will make it into the secret laboratory.

"Soil, Mae. Has there been some rift in the ground, or a landslide?" Sasha asks.

I think back to the five books in my father's hut. "There was a snow slide on the Benothian ranges. That was during the North and South divide, when Aldrych the First ruled. But then there was also a quake that split the ground near the Haedalands when Andrei ruled. I remember it now. Father said that his grandparents were born in the Haedalands not far from where the quake occurred."

"Well it must be the quake," Sasha says. "It's soil. The snow slide is frozen water. Everyone knows that."

I chew on my bottom lip. "But Aldrych is our current king's father. It would make sense to end the puzzle there. Snow isn't the same as soil, though. It can't be. It has to be Andrei."

"Mae," Sasha says. "Do you think Beardsley has rigged all the coffins? There are more than a dozen down here. What if you get it wrong?"

"I have to take the chance."

"So which king are you going with?"

Aldrych is close to the far wall where I suspect the entrance to the laboratory is, and Andrei is further back, near the poem. I turn to each, one after the other. There is a part of me that is drawn to Aldrych, even though the memory of the disaster during his reign is only partially related to soil, somehow I can imagine our king wanting to involve his father. A snow slide is more like a landslide than it is a tidal wave. I turn from Aldrych and head towards Andrei. No. The poem stated soil—I must go with the logical choice.

My palms are slick with sweat as I reach towards the hilt of the sword. I suck in the stale air of the underground crypt, and it is as though the walls are looming down around me, closing in tighter and tighter. My stomach clenches. I've been right so far. I press down on the hilt and it depresses into the coffin just like the others, and behind me there is the scrape of stone, as though a heavy door has been dragged open.

I spin around to Sasha in excitement. "I did it."

But Sasha's mouth is hanging open and her eyes are fixed on the ground. The sound of the scraping stone was not from the secret door at all. The final flagstone by the far wall of the crypt is pulled away, leaving a gaping hole in the ground. From inside that hole comes the sound of something scuttling and scraping.

"What is it?" I whisper.

Sasha shakes her head. "I don't know."

I take a step forward, hesitant to see what lies beneath the ground. There's a twist in my stomach that tells me this isn't the door we've been looking for. And as my heart pounds against my chest, a brass coated creature bursts from   the   opened   trap   door.

CHAPTER FOURTEEN

THE SECRET ROOM

It happens in a flurry of gold limbs. The creature leaps out towards me and I have barely enough time to summon wind to knock it back. As it staggers away I grasp hold of my sword and wield it in front of me, using both hands to steady the blade.

"What is it?" I shout to Sasha. But she is as still as the sarcophagi, staring at the mechanical beast.

It climbs to its feet and faces me. Ruby red glass eyes stare at me through the darkness. It has a long snout, a broad chest, four legs and a jaw full of sharp teeth. This time Beardsley has excelled himself, he has managed to create the most frightening dog I've ever seen. It snaps its jaw open and shut, imitating a dog gnashing its teeth, and even though it makes no such noise, I can imagine the growl at the back of its throat.

Sasha snaps out of her trance. "It has pieces of glass stuck on the end of its paws like claws, and there's a tail like a metal whip. It's very flexible and long, so be careful."

The dog scrapes its paws along the stone flags, as though waiting for the perfect time to pounce. In turn, I keep wind close to me, and hold my sword aloft. I'm limited in the amount of the craft I can use without endangering our lives down in the crypt. Water could end up drowning us, plus it would do little against the brass of the dog, flames would barely hurt the thing—not that I can create them anyway—and soil could end up in us buried alive. My best bet is to remember what Beardsley said about the spider—the weakness is in the eyes.

"Beardsley, for the love of the Gods, how did you make these things?" I mumble.

The dog sets off at a gallop and I push back with wind. I need to keep my power in check, controlling my emotions. The dog fights through the wind, but I manage to at least slow it down to give me enough time to pull back my sword and prepare to attack. As I withdraw my sword, ready to thrust it at the creature, the dog leans back on its hind legs and pounces towards me, its jaw open, the jagged teeth bare. I duck, swinging blindly with my sword, somehow managing a hit on the underbelly of the beast as I drop down to the ground. It at least throws the dog off course and it falls onto Andrei's coffin, knocking a chunk of marble from the corner.

I stagger back, onto the first highlighted flagstone. The brass dog lies unmoving on top of King Andrei, and I hope to all the Gods that it will not get back up. Then its head twitches to the right. Its tail flicks up and slaps against the stone. It gets back on its feet and turns to face me, only now one of its eyes have been smashed.

"Bash its head in, Mae," Sasha shouts. "I think it has some sort of... brain there."

The dog rushes towards me and sure enough behind that broken eye it seems as though there is a glint of something, a flash of an amber jewel like the amulets worn by the Borgans. I use the same tactic, slowing it down with a short, sharp gust of wind and then thrusting the sword forwards, letting out a cry as I throw my shoulder into the task. The dog tries to jump at me with its metal teeth showing, but this time I am ready for it, and I bring the sword down in a crashing blow on its last good eye. The dog is stunned, staggering back as it composes itself. That's when I ram the sword through its eye, managing to find a weak spot in the plates of metal at the back of its head. When I pull the sword back, it immediately goes limp. Sasha jumps up and down and cheers for me.

I reach down and collect the broken amulet. "Beardsley must have used amber because he knows it will channel the craft. Half mechanics and half magic. No wonder they are so terrifying."

"Mae!" Sasha calls.

I have barely enough time to face Sasha when three more brass dogs leap through the hole. I almost drop my sword at the sight of them. Sasha screams for me to go left, and at the last moment I'm able to move my limbs, missing the dogs by a hair.

The three dogs are identical, with the same powerful hind legs and sharp teeth. I try to ignore the nausea in my stomach and regain my balance, lifting the sword to protect me. The dog closest to me is the quickest to change direction, and it chases me down with sweeping strides. Air pulses from me, knocking the dog back and taking the other two with it, but the effort of using my powers in such force brings beads of sweat out on my forehead. My legs begin to tremble. If I'm not careful, I will weaken.

There's no way I can fight all three with a sword. Instead, I need to think fast. I need to outwit them. What is their weakness? I can't find any weakness at all. They are strong, fast, impenetrable. But then, I destroyed the first dog because it crashed into the sarcophagus. The dogs are not alive, that means they have no fear. They don't see hazards in the way humans and animals do.

With renewed energy, I position myself next to Andrei's tomb, silently apologising to the long dead king for desecrating his final resting place.

"I'm alive, Andrei," I whisper, never taking my eyes from the red glassy eyes of the dogs, "and I plan to stay that way."

As soon as I plant my feet, the dogs race towards me.

Sasha yells my name, but I do not look at her. Instead, I watch the path of the dogs, waiting. Waiting for the very last minute when all three have their legs lifted from the ground. And then I drop to my stomach. There's the clash of metal on stone behind me as I slither across the ground away from them. Shards of metal fall on me, one cuts through the cloth of my tunic, grazing my arm.

"Hurry, Mae. One of them is still functioning," Sasha warns.

I jump back to my feet just in time to raise my sword. The dog's jaw clamps down over the blade, and its paws hit me on the shoulders, knocking me back. Somehow, I lift my feet and kick its belly, managing to make the dog lose its balance. The dog's jaw loosens and I manage to retract the sword in time to make one last swing at its head. Something deep within me snaps and I hear a feral battle cry come from somewhere deep inside me. Primitive. Linked to fear and anger and the tenacity to survive. I haven't come all this way to be defeated by a metal dog.

The sword shatters the glass of the eye and penetrates the mechanism behind it, destroying the skull of the dog. Plates of metal fly through the air and the dog's body falls limp, hitting me with a thud. I have to heave it off me before I can stand, my entire body shaking.

"Wow," Sasha says. "You just killed *four* of those things. That was incredible."

The crypt is littered with broken glass and metal plates. I bend down and retrieve one of the amber coloured gems from the flagstones and put it in my pocket.

"I hope that's the last of them, because honestly, I don't think I could do that again." I stare down at my sword, mangled and bent from the metal on metal clash. My shoulder sings with pain from the effort of driving the weapon into the mechanical dog. I throw the contorted weapon onto the floor—now useless—and stretch out my sore back. "Right so, I'm guessing that was the wrong king."

Sasha laughs. "I think you might be right. But, look, the stones are still highlighted by light, that means you just have to press Aldrych I and we should be let in."

I wipe away the sweat on my forehead with the sleeve of my tunic. "But what if I'm wrong? I'm not sure now."

"Go through the options logically," Sasha suggests.

My eyes follow the two lines of sarcophagi. There are too many kings. What if I am missing something? I cannot think of any more quakes or landslides or anything relating to soil that would have impacted a king's rule. All I can think about is that avalanche in the Benothian ranges, the one that killed hundreds of Aldrych's men.

"I wish Father was here," I whisper, not realising I had said it out loud. My cheeks burn as I look sideways at Sasha.

"You can do this alone, Mae. You have a gut instinct that you can trust. You are the craft-born. You're magical. You should trust yourself," she says.

"I'm not alone," I reply. "Not when you're here. Although, it would have been nice if you could have fought those dogs."

She grins. "Sorry. But look how well you did. Mae, you know in your gut that the answer is Aldrych. Do it."

I shake my head and stride over to the last sarcophagus, the one nearest the far wall. "That's easy for you to say, you can't get your throat ripped out by a mechanical guard dog."

Before I press the hilt, I run my hand over the smooth marble. This is the newest addition to the crypt. Our current king's father. A shudder passes through me as I think of his body just inches away from my hand. It has to be him. It has to be.

I close my eyes as I press down on the sword, praying to anyone and anything, any God that might want to listen, that I am choosing the correct answer. The familiar scraping of stone against stone breaks the silence in the crypt. When the sound stops, Sasha gasps.

"Mae, you have to see this."

I open my eyes and turn. The crypt wall has opened up to reveal the secret room. At last. I run my fingers through my hair and let out a relieved laugh.

"We were right! We found it. We passed all the tests and we found it," I say, breathless with excitement.

But I need to curb my excitement, because we don't yet know *what* we have found. Sasha motions for me to go first. I retrieve a torch from the wall and step through the doorway into the room.

The first sight that hits you is the huge, cylindrical machine towering up several floors. It sits atop a great furnace in the middle of the room. All around the walls of the room runs a circular bench covered in test tubes and paraphernalia I've never seen before.

"This is all very strange." Sasha almost floats around the room, taking in the many bottles of potions, salts, rocks and stones laid out on the bench. "Mae, come take a look at this." Her voice is quick and breathy enough to make me hurry to her side. Once there, she points out a number of tiny black stones.

"What are these?" I lift one between finger and thumb to examine it. The dim light of the lantern, and the light from the one tiny window high up on the wall, bounces off the many facets of the stone. "I think this is a diamond."

"But it's black," she says. "Diamonds are transparent."

I've never seen a diamond in my life. I hide my embarrassment by snapping. "Well, it's some sort of jewel."

Sasha ignores my tone and leans towards the gem, squinting. "No, I think you were right. I remember when there were rumours going through the realm. We were ransacking a village outside Fordrencan. In the tavern, before we ambushed a couple of noblemen, there was talk of the King's debts. Someone said he'd been trying to make diamonds without the craft. Your magic doesn't just filter down to the amulets used by the Borgans, it can be harnessed by the Red Palace—"

"Yes," I say. "Beardsley told me all about that. He said that he built the machines to run from the energy my magic creates. But how does it make diamonds?"

"Well, they said it was to do with pressing something really hard until it makes it into a jewel. I don't know what it was, some sort of stone or something. He said the king was trying to make a black diamond because they are worth more."

"Well," I say, twirling the diamond between my fingers. "It looks like he succeeded."

Sasha purses her lips as though something is bothering her.

"What is it?" I ask.

"I don't know," she says. "It just seems a bit odd to keep all this hidden away. I mean, the entire realm knows about the diamonds."

"Maybe it's to stop people stealing them," I suggest.

"No," she says. "I think there's more to it. They have safes in the palace. It must be something to do with the contraptions they have down here."

"You mean, that," I say, pointing to the monstrosity in the middle of the room.

We both step closer, examining the strange machinery. Nothing seems particularly out of the ordinary, but then neither of us know the first thing in regards to technology. We've both lived in areas that are less advanced than Cyne.

"Why don't we try reading the King's

journal again," I say. "I still think he's crazy, but it might reveal something we've missed."

I find a chair to sit down. Fighting the dogs has weakened me, and I need a rest. But as I lower myself onto the seat, I find a sinking feeling pulling me deeper and deeper. As I go, I hear Sasha shout *Mae*, and:

I am the final story.
I am the fate of all.
I come too early for some.
Too late for others.

Craft-born, you will help me change my fate, or I will speed up the ending to your final story. If you help me, in return, I will give you the one thing you want in this world.

Then nothing.

CHAPTER FIFTEEN

THE NOTHING

The room is cold. There is a faint waft of mildew, indicating that I might be deep underground. Perhaps I am in the dungeon, the place criminals are left to rot, or the crypt again. My nerves tighten. The darkness is thick enough to consume everything in its path. I cannot see my hand, not even when I press my palm to my nose. Through that ever reaching darkness is one sound. Sobbing.

"Hello?" I say.

The sobbing continues, and a cold chill runs through my veins. It's too *personal* listening to someone cry like that. I take a tentative step forward, splaying my hands out before me so that I can feel my way in the dark.

"Is there someone here?"

The sobbing never breaks. The further I walk forwards, the more difficult it is to ascertain which direction the sound is coming from. Whenever I change direction, the crying does as well.

"Cas?"

My heart beats harder against my chest. Cas is the person I least want to find making such a wretched noise. The sobbing intensifies into a high-pitched wail causing a shiver to run down my spine. My breath exhales faster, panicked. I have to calm myself. It's just the dark and that crying making me frightened. There's nothing here to suggest I am in danger. At least not yet.

I stumble on, with my hands out ready to catch me if I fall. My feet shuffle against the cold stones below, only audible in the quieter moments of the crying. I have to force myself to focus on my steps. If I don't, I could find myself falling into a deep panic, unable to move at all. Part of me wants to stop walking, sit on the ground and rock back and forth until it's all over.

My eyes still have not adjusted to the dark. There is not a glimmer of light to be seen. I have no matches, and no lantern.

This time, I have the words of the Nix in my mind. *I will speed up your final story.* A threat— the first one. I take a deep breath and attempt to quell the tremor in my fingers. Now, I know it isn't a trick. The Nix wants me for a purpose—*to change my fate*—and until I have fulfilled that purpose, I am safe, at least from death. Pain on the other hand...

The sobbing turns to moaning. Then it quietens into a sniffling cry.

I stop and stand still, with a heavy feeling in my stomach. "Father?" The word escapes my throat in a rasp.

There is something about the place I am in, roughly the blackest black I have ever seen. Rather than dark it is devoid of all light. A nothingness. It panics me, seizing hold of my chest with an icy fist. What if the crying is my father? What if he is not at rest but trapped in some eternal state of... *nothingness.*

"Can you hear me?" I say. There is a quaver in my voice that cannot be disguised. I can't bear the thought of my father being left in a place like this. "Father?"

The unease spreads through my veins. How could I possibly defend myself in this darkness? I suck in a deep breath and try to calm the panic. Allerton told me to call on my powers before fighting. He's right. I should play to my strengths. I gather power at my sides and feel the wind collecting around me.

If only I could create fire. I would be able to light the way, I think.

Fire comes from anger.

I stand still and cup both hands in front of me. I cannot see them, but I imagine them, and concentrate on that image. I clench my fists three times and try to muster the kind of anger I felt when I watched my father's funeral pyre burn along the river. My skin prickles with the memory of the heat on my face, and the way the flames danced in the air.

I don't have to be that person again, I only have to learn to pretend to be her.

The thought gives me comfort. I can tap into that rage, but control it. Only, as I begin to let the emotions flow into me, I let in the grief, too.

But right now, the fear is worse than grief. Fear that my father is trapped in this place. Trapped in pain and suffering. That fear is more motivating than anything I have felt before.

"I'm in grief all the time anyway," I say aloud through gritted teeth. "I have to do this."

I don't have a choice. And yet, the grief still blocks me. I do not want to feel the same anger

I felt watching my father's body float down the river in Halts-Walden. Yet I must.

Without light I will never find out who it is trapped here. I will never know if it is Father. Tears spring at the back of my eyes.

This is a vision, I say to myself. *It isn't real.*

But as Sasha said, they are based on some truth. Some fundamental truth.

The sobbing breaks the silence once more. It seems to echo around me, like three or four voices at once. I spin around, breathing rapidly, dizzy from the fear and panic in my heart.

I focus myself, concentrating on the things I know. I cannot beat the Nix without tapping into this one last power. And now I have a choice, I can continue to stumble on in the dark, or I can dig deep and force myself to use this one last power.

Concentrate.

Father.

Fire.

Endwyn.

Anger.

I close my eyes and let it burn me. It begins as uncomfortable and intensifies into painful. The rage floods me, seeps through me. It's an emotion I have blocked because I saw how destructive it was, and it pains me to tap into that anger once more. I let out a cry of frustration and tears flow from my eyes.

The fire builds up from my gut. The heat runs through my veins like a lit fuse. A light film of sweat builds on my forehead, and I know I have to fight to control it. I have to use all my strength to stop myself exploding like a bright comet in the sky. My cheeks burn with the effort, but I control my breathing.

I open my eyes.

The fire bursts from my fingers like a flash of lightning. It's like a waterfall cascading out of me, lighting the entire room.

Except it isn't a room at all.

With an enormous fireball between my hands, I survey the scene around me. I know I don't have much time before I lose control of the fire and am forced to put it out. I examine all around me in a quick glimpse, my head moving in furtive, jerky movement. All I know, is that I am in an expanse; an expanse of nothingness—just as I had feared.

Everything around me is either black or grey. The floor is stone, but there are no flags like in the Red Palace. Instead, it stretches out like a never-ending lawn of flat grey. Instead of walls there is simply darkness.

But there is one outlying object in the complete stretch of nothingness. There is a man.

"Father!"

I rush towards him, but it takes me only a few moments to realise that he is not my father at all. He is someone else that I know, someone I did not expect to see.

I hardly recognise him at first. He is in tattered clothing. His face is a pallid grey and he lies flat on his back. There is no life in his features, and his cold grey eyes stare up, glassy. His mouth hangs open. It takes me only a moment to know that he cannot be crying. The sobbing cannot be coming from him in the same way it comes from all of us, it cannot come from his dead throat. Instead, it comes from his mind. I hear the pain in his mind. Or his heart. His soul.

The dead man in the expanse of nothingness is the King, and the sight of him makes my stomach roil with disgust. My fireball threatens to explode. I work fast to think of water—rain, rivers, the soothing of anger, calm. It is quicker to answer my call than the fire, perhaps because I want desperately for the darkness back so I no longer have to look at those eyes.

When Sasha watches me wake, the first thing I notice is the scrunched up expression on her face.

"Where did you go?" she asks before I can even draw a breath.

When I fell into the vision, I also fell off my chair, and the back of my head throbs. However, after examining it with my fingers, I'm relieved to find that there is no blood, just a small lump. I scramble up to my feet and sit back down on the chair with some caution.

"It was another vision from the Nix. This time I was in a long, stretched room and it was dark. I couldn't see an inch in front of me. But I summoned fire—"

She gasps. "You did? That's... that's incredible!"

"I almost blew myself up, but I summoned fire to see where I was going..." I trail off and pick at a thread in my tunic. "Sasha, I don't ever want to feel like that again. Summoning fire released some sort of rage inside me. It was *painful*... it was... disturbing."

"What happened?" she insists.

"I needed to light the way, because I thought... I thought my father might be there.

But then, when the fire burst from me, I realised it was someone else," I say. My voice sounds distant and quiet. "I saw him lying there. And he was sobbing. But there were no tears on his face. He wasn't making the sound from his throat. It was as though the noise came from deep within himself."

Sasha makes a tutting sound with her mouth, clearly frustrated with my vague reply. "But *who* did you see?"

"The king," I reply. "I saw the king lying on the ground. He was dead, I'm sure of it. His eyes were unfocussed, unblinking. His chest did not rise and fall. I only saw him for the briefest of moments and yet what I saw chilled me... deep down." I shudder as the ice cold passes through me once more.

Sasha quietens. She crosses her arms around her chest and stares down at the ground as though deep in thought. "How do you know it wasn't someone else crying in the room?"

"It wasn't a room," I say. "It was like an expanse of nothingness. And I don't know for certain, except that I felt as though I was in his mind. And I felt the same fear, the same dread of nothingness, like when you're laid in bed at night and wonder if the afterlife exists at all. That kind of fear. I think the king is afraid of dying, and I think that is how his fear manifested. Or, at least, that's how the Nix showed me the vision."

"All of this comes back to those two, doesn't it?" Sasha says. "The Nix, and the king. From the king's journal, to the secret laboratory, to the visions from the Nix... they must connect somehow."

"Yes," I say. "The Nix threatened me before I fell into the vision. It said that I need to find something to change its fate or it would speed up my final story, whatever that means. And in the king's journals he is frightened of something. Whatever he is frightened of, he wants Beardsley to fix it. Well, now we know it is death."

In that instant, all the pieces fall into place. The dark despair written in the king's journal, the pressure put on Beardsley to find an answer, the quest for magic to be brought back to the realm, and now his deepest fear is revealed...

"Death," I say again, thinking aloud. "Of course... it all makes sense now."

"Explain."

"Do you remember the old legend concerning the Ember Stone?"

I sing:

For many gaze up at the elder tree,
And yearn for immortality.
The old king searches far and wide,
But the Ember Stone will ever hide.

"When Mummers came to Halts-Walden they sang that song. Legend says that the key to immortality is in the finding of a mystical black diamond. There are people who search far and wide, in the mines of the Haedalands and the peaks of..." I stop when I see how Sasha's expression has turned very white.

"It isn't a diamond," she says. "It's an amulet. The Borgans know about it."

"They do? The legend is real?"

"The legend is very real. It is a black stone set into a necklace. Little is written on the subject. They say it was created by an ancient king but was lost. He used it to live forever. It's written in the craft-born journals."

"Where was it lost?" I ask.

She shrugs. "Nobody knows. It's all second hand knowledge and based on stories and songs."

"So how do you know it really exists?" I ask.

"Because we worship it. In a sense, anyway. Our amulets are a tribute to the great Ember

Stone. We fashion them from amber and it harnesses the power of the craft-born. Of course, they are nowhere near as powerful as the original."

"What would happen if the king found the Ember Stone?"

Sasha raises her eyebrows. "He would be the most powerful king that ever existed. He would be able to use your craft. He would be invincible, too. No forged weapon could kill him. No disease or infection could harm him. He would live forever."

I shudder at the thought. "The king is hoping he can recreate the amulet. He thinks that it's the diamond quality that could contain magical powers. That's why he's draining the resources in Cyne to keep the Red Palace production going. It's not for riches, it's for eternal life," I say. I hold up one of the tiny jewels between my finger and thumb and stare at the faceted gem in awe. How can one stone grant someone eternal life? I can only imagine the power inside it.

"You know what this means, don't you?" Sasha says. "This is worse than we ever anticipated. He would rule as a tyrant forever."

"So would the Nix. Allerton told me how it contains the fears of its ancestors and how frightened it is of dying. If the Nix will one day die of old-age or disease, I think it would want to do anything in its power to stop that," I say. "And when rumours travelled around Aegunlund about the king trying to make diamonds, the Nix must have decided to listen in on the king's thoughts. It has that power, right?"

Sasha nods.

"That's why it's trying to manipulate me," I continue. "How else would a giant slug like the Nix manage to achieve something so delicate? It wants me to find the Ember Stone and harness its powers. Then the Nix will manipulate me into handing it over. That's why it cursed my friends. That's why it's wearing me down with these constant visions. It wants me weak and disorientated when I find it. That way I'm easier to manipulate." I jump up from my chair. "But that means we must be close. The amulet must be somewhere in the Red Palace. We need to look!"

"Don't make any hasty assumptions," Sasha replies. "We don't know that the king has it." She lowers her voice. "Perhaps the Nix only *thinks* he has it. Mae, consider this for a moment, the Nix is a large physical creature, one who is strong and powerful. But what it relies on is not its body, but its powers. The Nix has the ability to see thoughts. But thoughts are not always reliable. They are jumbled and confusing. You've read the King's journal, you know for yourself. What if the Nix has been too hasty? What if the Nix hoped to find the Ember Stone before the king harnessed its power, and laid a trap to do so, but that trap came too early."

"What makes you think the king doesn't have the amulet?" I ask.

"Nothing concrete," she says. "Only, why would he still fear death?"

I let out a long sigh. "We can't trust the visions. We can't trust *anything*. I just wish we had some sort of proof. Or even a lead to go on. How am I going to free them?"

"We'll find a way," Sasha says. Her eyes narrow and she juts out her chin in defiance. "The Nix will not get away with this. We're going to stay here, and formulate a plan that ends with you scorching it like a chicken over a campfire."

"Sasha, I can't rely on fire. I managed it once, but I'm not sure I can do it again. The visions are different because it's as though my inhibitions are lowered. I know deep down it isn't real. Or maybe it's because the fear motivates me. I think we need a back-up, just in case." I don't say what's really on my mind, that I don't ever want to lose control like that again.

Sasha's eyes flash. "I have an idea!"

CHAPTER SIXTEEN

THE SIHRANS

"Are you ready?" Sasha asks.

I'm not sure that I am, but then I'm not sure I ever will be for what I am planning to do. There's no guarantee it will work. I don't care. I've lived under the assumption that nothing is guaranteed. Not even my life. Not that it matters. This is more important than me. If I can accomplish what I must do, it could make Aegunlund a safer place for us all.

"Do you really think this will work?" I ask.

Sasha chews on her lip. "I hope so, Mae. Just remember what we discussed. You're the one with the power, here. You're the craft-born. The Nix is just funnelling some of *your* magic to run the curse. That means you can control your surroundings just as easily as the Nix can. It's like the soul rip. You brought me here without even thinking. You can disconnect your spirit the same way. All you need to do is think where you want to go, and then you can gain control."

I nod. "Then I must use all my concentration."

I glance at the entrance to the laboratory. We should be safe inside the false wall, hard and unyielding brick, controlled by a lever inside the room. However, I can't shift the anxiety of voluntarily leaving Sasha alone while I attempt this task. Both of us wish Sasha was able to touch and feel, but as it is, she cannot defend us, and I worry that she can somehow be hurt like I was in the visions. What else can I do? This is what we have to work with.

"How do you know it will lift the curse?" Sasha asks.

"It has to," I reply. "This is the only way I can think to do it. The key has always been the fears. That's how it takes control. If I can break through the fears I can weaken it."

Sasha nods. "And if that doesn't work, you've summoned fire before. You can summon it again. You just need to believe in yourself."

I sit down on the small nest I've made out of the few cushions in the laboratory. Sasha sits next to me.

"Will you sing?" I ask. "While I'm gone, will you sing? I think it will soothe me while I'm there."

"Of course I will," she replies.

Her voice is high and melodic, twisting and turning. She tells a tale of love in a ballad so sweet it could soothe me into a gentle sleep. My muscles relax one by one. First my fists unclench, then my abdomen loosens. My breathing steadies. My throat is no longer closed. I inhale deeply and concentrate on the task ahead.

As soon as I lay my head against the pillows, the familiar sucking sensation drags me into a vision. But this time there is no riddle. There is no taunting voice in my mind. I am in control.

It's a sunny day in Halts-Walden and I'm sitting by the mill. My skin is pale as milk, and my skirt spreads across the green grass. I'm Ellen. But this time I am in control. I can lift my arms. I can stand and walk. I can even control her thoughts.

When Alice walks along the green lawns of Halts-Walden, my heart surges with joy. I stand up and take her by the hand.

"What are you doing?" she says, her wary eyes meeting mine.

"I need you to come with me and see my father," I reply. "There's something I need to say to him."

The birds chirrup in the neighbouring trees as the water cascades through the mill. It is a stunning day, one that makes me appreciate the beauty of my home village. A few weeks in the polluted city of Cyne has made me realise how much I miss it. But I don't ache for it, and I don't miss some of the narrow-minded people who shunned me for being different.

Being in Ellen's body made me realise that we aren't really that different from each other. We both had a secret hidden deep down, one that could change our lives forever. I hope, from the bottom of my heart, that Ellen is in this vision somehow, that she will see what I do, and I hope it gives her the strength to do the same.

My hand reaches out to the door knob to the small cottage where the Millers live. My heart begins to pound. What if this doesn't work? And just as the doubts creep in, so does the one sound that can make me go cold all over: *click-ick-ick-ricker*.

"The Nix," I whisper.

"The what?" Alice asks.

"Nothing."

I must keep concentrating, and keep control of Ellen's body. I can feel her pulling away. No, this must come from deep within. It must be rooted in my powers in order for it to work. I take a deep breath and step into the kitchen.

Ellen's mother is stirring broth. She looks up from her work, and her eyes widen in surprise. "Oh, hello dear. Are you coming in for some lunch? We have broth—"

"Where's father?" I hate to be rude, but I need to focus, and to get it done as soon as I can.

But I needn't have asked, because he strides in from the washroom, his hair damp and dishevelled from the water.

"What's going on?" he asks, eying Alice with some suspicion.

"I have something to announce to you both," I say, straightening my back. There's a little voice at the back on my mind which knows what I am about to do. It knows, and it is terrified. It screams for me to stop. "I am in love with this girl."

Alice gasps. "Ellen, what are you doing?"

"I am in love, and there is nothing you can do to change me," I continue. A cold sweat breaks out on my forehead as the Ellen within me protests against what I'm doing. "I don't care what you think. I don't care if you think it's wrong."

Alice wrenches her hand from mine and disappears through the open door. Seeing her go causes Ellen's heart to twist. I wince and turn away from her. This isn't real. It's just a vision. But I need to remember that I can still be hurt.

The miller stands with his mouth open wide. His wife is quietly sobbing into her dress sleeves. I'm waiting for him. I know his next action and I'm waiting for him, but Ellen is terrified. Her knees are trembling, and tears are close to erupting. She wants to fall to his feet and beg for forgiveness.

I won't let her. I am in control now.

"What is this insolence?" he says at long last. "How dare you speak these things in my house?"

"I'm only telling you the truth, father," I say.

He takes a step forward, and Ellen's body jumps back away from him. I struggle to regain control and stop her from fleeing the scene. Her fear is trying to take over, but I won't let it. This is *my* vision now. Not one controlled by the Nix. I force her to face her father and jut out her chin in defiance. Seeing this enrages him further, and he slaps her hard around the face. I feel the sting as though it was my own skin. Ellen's mother whimpers into her sleeve.

After the initial shock from the pain of the slap, I gather control, pull my arm back, and hit Ellen's father squarely on the chin. Inside, Ellen—wherever she may be—celebrates.

But then, the miller comes at me with the same look of rage in his eye that I remember from Ellen's first terrifying vision. This is it. This is the moment where I can break through. I watch him, following his movements as he lurches towards me, and duck away from him. In an instant I am by the fire, picking up a heavy poker to defend myself with.

The miller cowers away from me, raising his hands in front of his face.

"Stop," he says. "Please stop."

His wife watches with her jaw hanging open in shock. "Ellen what are you...?"

I begin to lower the poker, when the miller

jumps to his feel and lunges towards me. I have only a few seconds to duck away from him. The sight of his dark eyes will haunt me for a long time.

Now, I raise the poker higher. But as I plan to strike down on him, part of Ellen takes control. She turns to her mother.

The miller's wife's mouth is contorted in rage and there is a shiver that passes through Ellen's body as she seems to prepare herself for her mother to join in the attack with her father. But then the miller's wife narrows her eyes and nods.

"Do it," she says.

Ellen and I have a mutual control which is thrilling to be part of. We both enjoy bringing the poker down on her bully of a father.

The vision dissipates, and I am with Beardsley back in the tunnels of the castle. He is mumbling to himself, and running the sleeves of his robe through gnarled old fingers.

I turn on my heel, forcing him to look at me.

"The king has employed you to create a false black diamond, hasn't he? He has forced you to use this castle for his own nefarious plot, and he wanted the magic of the craft-born to try and force his diamonds to give him immortality," I say.

Beardsley's milky eyes lift up to mine. "But how did you…? Who told you…?"

"I figured it out of course. I am no fool. You need to face up to what you have done, old man. If you don't, you'll regret it."

"Yes," he says, his eyes unfocussed and confused. "The tunnel. It will never end if I don't, and the spiders will be waiting for me, just like the bodies of all the people my weapons will kill. There will be many, you know. So many. I never had a daughter, but if I'd had one, I would have liked her to grow up like you." He pats me on the head like I am far younger than my years, but I don't mind. "Strong head, strong heart."

My cheeks burn as he utters the same words as Allerton. Are they true? Am I capable?

"You must believe it," he says. "Believe it and you will do it. Now, if you will excuse me, I'm going to go and feed myself to the spiders."

I open my mouth to protest, but it's then that I realise I should not be preventing this. I need to let Beardsley go. That is how I defeat this fear, not by fighting it for him, but by allowing him to be consumed by it. Only then will he move on from the guilt.

Click-ick-icker-ick.

It's like cold molasses spreading over my skin. The Nix is somehow encroaching on *my* visions, it is trying to force its way in. I need to hurry. We both turn back in unison to see a jet of serum travelling towards us. Now it is appearing in its own visions, attempting to stop us from breaking the curse.

"Run!" I shout.

We hurry down the tunnel, with Beardsley shuffling as fast as he can.

"It's no good," Beardsley says. "We can't outrun it."

I glance back to see, with a heavy heart, that he is right. It seems unlikely that I will be able to fight against the Nix and keep Beardsley from coming to harm at the same time. I don't know what would happen to him, seeing as it is a vision, but I don't want to find out. The Nix being here breaks the rules of the last few visions, which indicates that anything could happen.

But perhaps the breaking of the usual rules can work in my favour. Sasha's words pop into my mind. I can take control. I can use my powers and change the outcome of the vision.

"Beardsley, take my hand," I say.

He reaches across and I grab hold of his old bones. Another spray of serum comes towards us. If it touches us, we could be paralysed and under the Nix's control. Now is the moment where I need to take the control back. I think of Beardsley and his spiders. I think of the castle and its layout.

The serum is a whisper from my arm and I turn my head a fraction to see the teeth of the Nix in close proximity.

"Hold on," I whisper half to myself.

The venom, the Nix, and the darkness of the tunnel fade away, and we end up running straight into a hung tapestry in one of the palace hallways. Beardsley collapses to his knees, wheezing. I look around me. I've transported us to a separate part of the castle, away from the Nix.

"I'm sorry, old man," I say. "It was the best I could do."

"You're the craft-born," he replies. "I should have known."

"Yes," I say. "But it doesn't matter. You probably won't remember when you wake up anyway."

"What was that creature? Was it another one of my creations?"

"No, it was after me," I reply. "It is trying to control me so that I will give it immortality. The king isn't the only one searching for the

Ember Stone."

Beardsley sucks in another deep breath. "I never said this to the king because he would probably have me executed, but I don't actually believe that the craft can be inserted into a regular, man-made diamond. I've managed to harness many contraptions throughout the palace based on craft magic, but this is something different. This is beyond any magic in the realm today, even yours. The Ember Stone was made by the Ancients. By one of the most powerful Ancients, actually. It possesses the purest magic that has ever existed. But the diamond has long been lost."

"According to the Borgans an old king had it made. It was lost somewhere." I shake my head. "I had always thought that it was just a story."

"Oh, it's real." Beardsley lets out a heavy sigh. "Before the king asked me to create false diamonds, he searched far and wide for it. He had men in the Haedalands mines, and even in the Southern Archipelagos. He sent a team towards the mountains in the North, too. But he never found a lead. Only dead ends. That was when he had the idea to create a new one from craft magic, and forced me into helping him. I never wanted that terrible man to rule the realm into the ground as an immortal, but I am a fearful man who is weak. I worked for him regardless. But Mae, there is something you should know."

"Tell me. Quickly," I say.

"When I realised making diamonds would never amount to anything, I began to do my own research. I found texts written by the Ancients. They were in the Aelfen language, but I managed to translate some. I couldn't translate it all, but I managed at least some. There is reason to believe that the Ember Stone is hidden in a temple beneath the Anadi sands."

"*Beneath* the Anadi sands?" I repeat.

He nods.

"But, how?" I reply.

"Long ago there was a tribe of Aelfens called the Sihrans who resided in the Anadi sands. They lived in temples and were very holy. They dedicated their lives to worshipping the God of magic, Dwol. As a reward for their dedication, the God imbued his power upon their leader and that power flowed into the Ember Stone. It was said to be the most stunning diamond in all of Aegunlund. I think this tribal leader could be the king your Borgans were talking about."

"What happened to them? Why is it now below the sands?"

"There was a great sandstorm and the tribe were buried in it."

"But they were immortal? How did they die?" I ask.

Beardsley's eyes shine. "Who said they died? There is a chance that buried deep under the Anadi sands is a tribe of people still living. They could be sleeping, they could be somehow conscious, I don't know. Or it could all be a rumour and they could have truly perished. But it certainly warrants investigation."

"Where are these texts? Where can I find them?"

"They are in my office, dear," he replies. "I keep the scrolls in a canister in my desk. Perhaps you should find them and conduct your own research. Something tells me I am not long for this world."

"Don't say that," I reply, aghast.

His old face nods slowly. He is grey: from his hair to his beard, to the pallor of his thin skin.

"Help an old man back on his feet," he says. "I am ready to face my inventions."

"Are you sure?"

"Quite sure. Come on. Up I must go."

Beardsley leans on me as he rises. I feel the frailty in his body.

"Good bye, Mae," he says to me, cupping my cheek with one hand. "You have reminded me that there is still good in the world. I believe we are on a constant scale of good and evil, and there are often slight dips either way. For a long time our world has been tipped further towards evil than good. But I believe you have been sent to us to balance those scales."

"No—" I begin.

"Yes, yes. Do not argue with an old man. You won't see it—not for a long time, perhaps—but you are a force in this world. Now, off to my spiders I shall go."

My eyes burn with unshed tears. I know this is what I need to happen in order to break the Nix's plans, but my gut twists with remorse. This vision feels too real. Part of me believes I will never see Beardsley again.

CHAPTER SEVENTEEN

THE VISION OF TEMPTATION

Psst. Psst.
  Click-ick-ick.
  The Nix.
  "Psst!"
  "Who's there?"
  A cacophony of sound bursts through the silence and the room spins and spins until I think I might throw up. A horrible corset digs into my ribs. There is music in the air, slow and melodic. People giggle and flatter each other, or glug down wine. Wig powder flurries to the floor as heavily rouged women take canapés from silver platters. Next to me, a little boy pokes his head around a gold embroidered curtain.

"Prince Casimir," I say, a smile coming to my lips. Those eyes haven't changed. They are still as open and kind as ever.

"Have you seen my brother? He's the tall brute with the whip."

I bend down to eye level with the little prince. "Now, you listen to me. You're worth ten of people like him. He is a bully because he is weak, and you should not be afraid of weakness. Never be afraid of someone's weakness, it's a waste, Cas, a waste of your energy. You should focus on your own strengths. You are a kind and gentle soul, and you should nurture that, because one day you will become king and you will need those qualities to be a good king."

"That doesn't stop him hitting me."

"Then you must think of one thing you are good at that he is not, and then use that one thing to your advantage."

Cas nods. "There is something. I'm faster." His eyes widen, he steps out from behind the curtain.

"That's good! You use that."

"What if he still wins?" Cas asks. His boyish eyes catch the light in the room.

"He isn't winning. As long as he remains a bully, no one will truly care for him. He will only frighten people into doing what he wants. That's no way to live. It's a *lonely* way to live."

Cas breaks into a smile. "Thank you." He moves out from behind the curtain and stands a little taller. "I will always remember you."

His words give me a chill, even though I know this is only a vision version of Cas, I feel as though he really will grow up to know me.

"Hey, how did you know my name?" he asks, his silver eyes narrowing.

"I, umm, well…"

The sucking sensation is back, pulling me away so I don't have to explain myself. That's three of the fears dealt with. Some seem easier than others. Most concern standing up to those who frighten us. I suppose I've never realised how afraid we are of other people.

This next fear is one I have dreaded. It is the queen's fear, the gruesome depiction of regicide and fratricide conducted by the disturbing Lyndon. It has not escaped my attention that I have never been inside Lyndon's deepest fear. Perhaps he doesn't have one. The Nix needs something personal to work with, and if there is nothing there, then there is nothing to show.

This time I am not in the queen's body and it is this time that I see her face as her son's head is dumped on top of her sheets. She struggles away from the dead eyes of her husband and collapses back onto the floor away from the bed.

"I can be king now, Mummy, isn't that what you've always wanted?" Lyndon says, in a sickly sweet voice that sends a shiver down my spine.

The queen's screams are frantic and terrifying, high-pitched and desperate. For a brief moment I want nothing but to disappear from that room, to leave the stench of death and blood-soaked sheets, and the sound of a mother screaming for her child. But I can't. I need to take control. I need to show the Nix that I am more than capable of taking control, and that my magic is stronger. He can control our minds, but only if we are weak. I am strong, and I will defeat him. I have to change this vision into a solution.

So I take a deep breath and I change the surroundings. Within seconds, the horrifying screams stop, replaced by new sounds: a baby crying and the panicked hushes of a mother trying to quieten him.

"This is for the best, this is for the best," the queen says over and over. I walk with her as she hurries down a corridor. She does not see me. It is as though I am invisible. "I must keep you away from him. It's the only way."

Her feet scuff against the stone floor, and in her haste she almost trips. She wears a cloak covering her face, and the baby is swaddled in a light grey woollen blanket.

"Your Majesty," comes a whispered voice. A man steps out from the shadows. He is dressed in britches and light armour. I recognise him as Finan, Cas's bodyguard killed by the Borgans in Halts-Walden. "I am here."

"You must take my son and ride far from here. I cannot say why I must do this, only that I know if I keep him near my husband, something terrible will happen. Do you trust me? It will mean going behind my husband's back. You will never be able to return to Cyne."

"I am your loyal servant, my lady." There is a glint in his eye that reveals a personal moment between the two of them, and I am glad that the queen has known at least some happiness while married to a tyrant.

"Good bye my little Lyndon. Grow to be the man I want you to be, not the man your father wants you to be."

I back away from the conspirators, pleased that I found a solution for the queen's fear. She finally admitted to herself that she believes her son is evil under the influence of the king, and she found a way to deal with it.

A sense of calm spreads over me. I close my eyes and let the smile come back to my lips. If only I could change real life, I could make sure everyone gets what they want. Perhaps even me?

But these solutions are temporary. As soon as I break the curse, all these fears will come back. Lyndon will still be in the Red Palace.

A cold dread seeps through my veins, thick as molasses. The image of Anta pops into my mind, and again I feel as though something bad is going to happen. This picture is somehow disconnected from the Nix, separate from the fears I have been treading. I can't explain why I know that, perhaps it is my connection to the craft, my gut instinct telling me, forewarning me. Both Allerton and Sasha tell me that the Nix likes to trick people, that it will show you distorted versions of the truth, and I must disregard anything I cannot control, yet there is a horrifying niggle in my mind that Anta is in *real* danger, and while I am stuck in this curse there is nothing I can do about it.

I shake my head, trying to force the image out of my mind. It is just the Nix trying to weaken me. I have been able to infiltrate his visions, to control them and stop the fear it spreads. The Nix feeds on fears, and while ever I control the fears, I stop the Nix from controlling me. That means I can stop myself from working for the Nix.

"It wants you to think you need it," I remind myself. "It wants you to believe that your loved ones will die without its assistance. That's why it keeps sending you into the fears. Control it, Mae." *A strong mind and a strong heart.*

I push my worries away, form fists at my side so tightly that my fingernails dig into my palms, and then I concentrate on going to my next destination.

Click-ick-icker-ick.

Where are you going, craft-born? The words appear in my mind, in the sickly voice of the Nix, making my skin-crawl. *What do you think you will achieve?*

"I'm going to defeat you once and for all. You can't control me anymore, I'm too strong." A searing pain rips through my skull and images hurtle through my mind. They are all of me and Cas: talking in the Waerg Woods, dancing in the ballroom, Cas alone on the bell tower after we talked about the sea, the kiss in the hidden tunnel... more, things I've never seen—a magical day where we walk hand in hand through a garden filled with flowers, Cas turning a bright silver ring on my finger and leaning forward to move stray hairs from my eyes, we're older and my stomach is swollen. He reaches out and places a hand on my belly...

"NO!" I shout. "Stop it. We will never have any of that. We can't be together—"

Because you lied to him.

I clamp my hands against my ears. "Shut up!"

He will never trust you now.

"I said shut up!"

You will lose him as a friend. Unless you help me. Help me find the Ember Stone and I will give you anything you want.

"No," I whisper. "You couldn't, you don't have the power."

The visions are easy, aren't they, Mae? Life is much simpler when you are in them. Your life with Cas could be like that.

"It would be a lie," I say. "I would be living a lie."

Before I can do anything more, I feel the familiar, dizzying sensation of being pulled through into another vision. I'm back in the tunnel. Cas's silver eyes burn bright through the darkness.

"We should go," he says. "We don't have much time."

"Where are we going to go?" I ask.

"Does it matter? As long as we are together."

"Why? Why do you love me?" I ask. His hands are on mine. They are warm and comforting, but grip hard enough to send tingles up my arms.

"Mae, you're like a whirlwind. You're passionate and free spirited and you never stand still. Life with you is an adventure. I want us to have our own adventures, away from here, away from these people... my father."

"But you were meant to be king. You would be a good king. "

"I don't want to rule and I never have. Deep down I never expected to make it to the throne. I always thought Lyndon or Father would finish me off by then. But you and me together, that is something I want. I'll get Gwen, you can find Anta, we'll ride down to the Haedalands and see the South Seas. It will be beautiful. Imagine the stretching yellow of the Anadi Sands. Don't you want to see it, Mae? Don't you?"

More than anything. To open my lips and say yes feels like the most natural response in the world. "Why is this your fear?"

"Pardon?"

Tears well in my eyes. "Why is this your greatest fear? Loving me frightens you. Why?"

"It doesn't frighten me," he says. He drops my hands and takes a step back. "I don't… I don't know what you mean."

"This is your fear, Cas, but I can't figure out what you are afraid of. Are you afraid of me? Or are you afraid of marrying someone you don't love? Or are you afraid of staying here and having to be king?"

Cas runs his fingers through his sandy-blond hair. "I don't know."

"Then we can't leave," I say. "You can't just run away."

He takes my hands again. "Yes, we can—"

"No, because none of this is real." I pull away from him. "It's not real. This is all… it's some sort of…"

"What are you talking about, Mae?"

"You have to go back." The tears run down my cheeks. "Go back and face your brother and your father and tell them that you will rule the kingdom and you will do a better job of it than they ever have or will. That's your destiny, Cas. It's not to be with me."

"I don't want any of that."

"You don't want it, but Aegunlund needs it. We need you. The people need you." *I need you.* The words are on my lips, but they remain unsaid. There is a lot inside of me that has remained unsaid, and probably always will.

"Is this what you want?" he asks, looking deep into my eyes.

I know that this isn't real. I know that the Nix has created this vision, and yet it feels authentic, like it is the greatest truth I have ever known. My body is burning with the desire to change course, to run away with Cas, and live in this world where he and I are together, even though our bodies lay sleeping in different parts of the Red Palace. It would be living a lie, but what a lie it would be!

I shake my head. And what happens when the Nix pulls me back? And I know it will. What happens then? I'll be weak, physically and mentally, at mercy to its will. By then it will have power over the kingdom, with the curse still fallen on the castle and the realm in disarray. The Nix wants me to choose this path. It wants me to fail. It wants me as its puppet, to use my powers to acquire the

Ember Stone and live forever, ruling the world into its dark version of hell.

"This is what I want, Cas," I say. "I don't want to go with you, I'm sorry. I just want to be alone."

Cas's jaw goes slack. "But I thought…" He straightens his back. "Very well, I saw something that wasn't there. And to think I almost tore myself apart with the guilt…" his voice fades away and he shakes his head. "I was so afraid of my own feelings that I never thought of what this moment would be like. I've been such a fool."

The tears spring into my eyes, thick and fast enough to drown in. "No, you are *not* a fool, and you never have been. Not even when we first met and I treated you as though you were. I just didn't know you. Once I knew your heart…" My voice breaks on the word heart.

"Well clearly not enough," he says, letting out a hollow little laugh. "Fine, if you say I will make a good ruler, then I will. Now I know that… Now this has been resolved, I can put all my efforts into becoming the king Aegunlund needs."

"I think that's for the best," I say.

"Still, it isn't safe for you here—"

"Don't worry, I won't stay. I… shouldn't

stay." Again, I forget that this isn't real. My bottom lip trembles as I force back tears. "I'll take Anta and go south."

"You still want to see the Haedalands?"

"Yes, I do."

"Very well. This is goodbye then."

"I guess it is."

Cas holds out his hand towards me in the formal way, but I push it aside and pull him close to me instead. At first he is rigid, but then he sinks into my embrace. I've taken him off guard, and I'm glad of it; it gave him no time to resist.

"Maybe one day we can meet, sometime in the future when all this madness has ended and we can sit by the sea and it will be like those campfires in the Waerg Woods."

"I would like that," he says.

And then he is gone. My arms are empty and I am left in nothingness.

Complete nothingness. Fear grips my heart as though in a vice. Where am I?

CHAPTER EIGHTEEN

THE POWERFUL AND THE WEAK

After a few moments of utter panic, I calm myself long enough to recognise my surroundings. The pitch black expanse. The nothingness. The death of the king. That wracking sob warbles out into the empty space. My eyes see as much open as they do shut, and my breath comes out in ragged gasps as I try to control the dread seeping over my skin.

"You're dying, aren't you?" I shout.

He falters, sucks in a breath, and then the crying continues.

"That's what this is all about. You're dying, and because you're afraid, you're taking it out on Aegunlund. You've orchestrated the laboratory in the Red Palace so that you can make your diamonds, and you have pulled me into your little scheme because you are desperate for the craft-born to reignite the powers in the castle. And all this time you have ruined your own land and polluted the air in order to create an Ember Stone. But you failed. You can't make an Ember Stone at all."

The crying stops. He lets out a succession of quick breaths.

"You are the most pathetic man I have ever known, and I have met many a wastrel in The Fallen Oak. What did Aegunlund do to you? Does it deserve the way you have treated it? Does it? Do the people deserve such a weak man for a king? You should step down and let Casimir take over, a fair and just man."

"Bah! He is weaker than I!"

"Only someone who cannot see beyond skin would say such a thing. Have you ever taken the time to stop and get to know your son? Well, have you? I think not. You did not see the fearless way he fought in the Waerg Woods. He was frightened at first, but only idiots have no fear. Real strength comes from being afraid and doing it anyway. The opposite of what you are doing right now. I have seen Cas look death straight in the face without flinching. I have seen him embrace his death. Not like his father, a sobbing, quivering mess—"

"You don't know!" he booms. "You don't know how I've lived, how I've suffered."

"Oh spare me. I do know. I have come close to death several times during my journey here, and, yes, I have flinched, I have fought, and I have almost failed more than once, but I never gave up, and I would never, ever, take another life in order to live longer. You have taken hundreds of lives to try and prolong yours. You have killed your own people to do it. You are a small man, a despot king, a man to be laughed at. I will kill you myself."

I step forward in the dark with my hands in front of my face. It is useless. The nothingness is so thick that I cannot see even an inch in front of my face. If I am to find the king I must use light. The only way I can do that is by conjuring fire. I gulp at the thought. That means releasing more rage.

"You'll have to find me first," the king growls.

"I am more powerful than you can imagine," I say. "And I will find you."

I stumble forward, holding out my hand

palm up. Despite my brave words, my fingers tremble. I'm not sure what I am more afraid of: summoning fire, or fighting the king. I shake my head and begin to let the anger burn within me. This is only a vision. It isn't real. I can use fire here, I've done it before. I must force my powers to my will. This is the only way I will learn.

"You silly girl—"

"No, not girl," I say. I have to stop and double over. The burning sensation ripping through my body causes real, physical pain. I let out a groan as I straighten my back and allow the fire to spring into action, glowing orange-red in the dark room, "craft-born." I force myself to stand upright, strong and tall.

I will not let the fire control me.

Somewhere in the distance there is a whimper and the scuttling of feet. The king has seen my fire, which means that he cannot be far. I draw my arm back and fling the burning flame away from me, searching for the cowardly man. The fire burns bright and travels far, but there is nothing to be seen, no corners, no corridors, just a vast expanse of nothingness.

Where is he?

My gut twists with pent up rage. It's like

bathing in hatred. I hate fire. I hate what it makes me feel.

I wish I could sweep the room in a systematic fashion, but without walls or corners, there's little I can do. I just keep moving forwards, throwing fireballs in all directions. They travel but never hit a surface. The king's fear seems impossible to navigate because it is nothingness.

"There has to be something," I mumble to myself. A trickle of sweat works its way down my temple. "No one can imagine nothingness. There has to be something, a trail, a pathway, something that he's added to this world."

I stare down at my feet. Perhaps the floor is the only clue in this world. After all, the king has invented the ground I'm walking on.

"Footprints!" I say.

Layers of dust have coated the expanse of the floor, and within the dust, there are the unmistakeable signs of boot prints. The king has left a trail of his attempted escape.

I slow my steps, placing my feet quietly onto the dust. I wrestle with the fire ball in my hand, controlling it takes all my concentration, but I manage to force it down to a candle flame. My control is improving, but the effort is draining. At least I'm doing it. Allerton was right to teach me the final element.

But still, the thought of killing with fire makes my throat close. There is something primitive about this element. I hurry on, wanting nothing more than to find the king and leave.

The silence becomes a suffocating blanket that highlights the sound of my own body. My breath becomes a hurricane; my heart is a beaten drum. I think for certain that the king can hear me approach. I imagine him crouched, waiting. Like a hunting cat engulfed in shadows.

I concentrate on my senses. There is no sound. He must either be still or moving very slowly. There is no sight of him. He is cloaked in the shadows of his world. But there is a smell. It's a very faint scent, one of musk, dried sweat and something else... like the tang of metal. It could be the smell of his chainmail or armour. Or his fear.

He's close.

My shoulder blades dampen with sweat as I think of how I will defeat the king. I could never take him in battle. He might be a pathetic sobbing mess, but he is still stronger than me in combat. I will need to use my craft-born powers.

I could consume him in fire, but the thought of watching a man die in the flames turns my stomach.

I could throw him against the wall with wind. A vision of his broken body hitting the wall with a sickening crunch causes my flame to die down to a mere flicker.

You cannot kill.

I've had more than one opportunity to kill a foe, and every time I have found another way. What if my doubts are correct? What if I cannot take a life? Back in Halts-Walden I couldn't even hunt.

Is there another way to break this fear? The king is afraid of dying, it makes sense to kill him and force him to face his fear. And it's not real. I must repeat this mantra. The Nix has constructed this reality. He has done it to test me, to weaken me. The only way I can break through is to remain strong and do what I must.

I must kill him.

I must.

There's a scrape and my head snaps in the direction of the sound. I enlarge the fireball in my palm and lift it into the air until it hangs suspended above my head. It's then he comes running out of the shadows, his chainmail chinking, his face contorted, his mouth gaping open, a battle cry escaping from his lips, his sword held high above his head.

I stagger back, tripping on my feet and tumbling to the floor. In that instant I am a little girl again. I am the pathetic little Mae who believes she is more daring than she really is; who demands adventure and then balks at danger. In a split second the sword is coming down on me, giving me one fleeting moment to roll from its path.

I jump to my feet, my pulse pounding; every single muscle tensed, ready to run.

But I can't.

I need to break this cycle.

As the king lunges for me again, I call on wind to throw him back.

His steps falter as the wind pushes him back. I blow a gale, forcing him to push through the wind. He leans forward with his hair blowing back, his eyes are pale fierce spheres locked on mine and determined.

"You may have little tricks up your sleeve," he says, "but you do not have the same passion to live. I will *not* face my end. I have not worked all this time to die at the hand of some Haedaland peasant girl."

I keep the wind on him, battering him with

my powers, but he pulls himself to his feet, staggering towards me, still with his sword held high. I can feel the gift diminishing from me, drawn out by mental drain. I've dipped into them too much too fast. As my powers weaken, the king grows stronger, coming ever forwards. He is right about one thing, he is determined to live. He has his fingernails plunged deep into the flesh of life and he refuses to let go; the tenacious grip of pure fear.

I drop the wind and snuff out the fire, running back into the shadows away from him, my body cold, clammy, trembling. My hands shake as I try to stay composed.

Now we cannot see each other at all.

I hear the king swing his sword, grunting with each stroke. I decide to use this opportunity to keep away from him and let him tire himself out. I need to recharge my powers.

"You won't escape me, peasant girl," he growls. "I will find you and I will cut you in half. I will not be defeated."

His voice is surprisingly close, prompting me to step back just in time. His sword swipes towards my arm, catching me with a shallow slice. The king realises this and comes closer, forcing me to turn and run away.

"I can hear you running," he says. "You little coward. You have a lot of big talk for a silly little girl from the Haedalands."

This is it. I need to use my powers. This time I manage to block out the full extent of the rage, but still find the fire come to me with ease. The fireball explodes from my hands. "I'm from Halts-Walden!" The release is incredible, like a rush of adrenaline I have never experienced before. It both exhilarates and frightens me in equal measure. I find that the pain of the anger and hatred has gone. It's such a relief that I laugh. This is how it should be. This is how my powers should work. Fire is now as easy as summoning wind. Why did I have such trouble?

The fire hits him squarely on the shoulder, causing the king to drop his sword. He panics, swatting himself with his other hand, trying to stop the fire from spreading. There is a sickening scent of burning flesh in the air, but I have not ejected enough to kill him.

While he is distracted, I bend down and retrieve his sword, leaving him unarmed.

As the fire goes out, I say, "And I am not a girl. I'm the craft-born, you should remember that."

There is a great roar, and before I can move away, the heavy beast of a man throws himself on top of me. His hands grip my wrist, attempting to wrestle the sword from me, but I hold it tight, pointing it upwards, somewhere near to where I imagine the king is.

I try to use wind to throw him from me, but the frantic nature of wrestling seizes me with a paralysing fear. I find myself scratching at his eyes with my free hand, while attempting to yank the sword from his grip.

We roll along the floor. A fist hits me on the side of my face, loosening a tooth and causing me to bite my tongue. Blood gushes into my mouth, metallic and warm.

I manage to knee him in the crotch and attempt to wriggle out from underneath him. He grabs at my thighs but I kick his chest, he lets out a cry and I scramble to my feet.

I prepare myself to invoke another fire ball, but the king is faster. With a great cry I feel his weight thrown at me again, but this time I have a tiny opportunity to angle the sword towards his chest. I grip the hilt with both hands and hold it fast as the king impales himself on his own sword. The deadly steel finds the weak spot between his armour, sliding up and under his ribs. All the way to his heart. With a sick feeling in my stomach, I push it that last inch, feeling the resistance of his flesh, and when I am certain that I have landed a fatal blow, I stagger back, with my hand over my mouth.

Through the darkness comes light, and it is not light I have created myself, it is a piercing light filling the nothingness. It shows the blood on my hands. It reveals the king falling to his knees with his eyes wide open in shock. I watch as the fear consumes him. I see the terror in those eyes.

My father's books told the history of the kings, but that spoke even more about war. I've heard soldiers called heroes. Men fight for glory, but there is no glory in taking a life, only a sick feeling that churns at your stomach. In that instance you are terrified of your own power. You are aware of what we all have inside of us—the ability to kill. No matter how good you are or how sensitive, you can kill. I discover that in the moment the king falls onto his back with his unfocussed eyes staring up at me, still terrified.

I'm sick. I throw up onto the dusty floor of the king's vision.

I never wanted this.

But somehow I took the responsibility I didn't want, and I claimed it as my own.

After I'm sick, I cry.

What is it about our lives that make us feel so formidable one moment and so weak the next? Even in moments of pure power we find our true weaknesses.

I stagger back from the corpse and turn away. The last fear. I've been through them all and I have destroyed each and every one of them. If the Nix feeds on the fears of its victims, surely I have done enough to weaken its powers and break the curse. I need to leave this place. The Red Palace should go back to normal. The king will wake up and be alive. I need that reality now. I need it to happen.

But it would seem there is one last vision for me to walk through.

CHAPTER NINETEEN

THE BLACK CROWN

I am in a room I have only ever peeked into before. It is the throne room, a place where the king is supposed to sit and listen to the woes of his subjects. According to the rumours spread amongst the servants, the king spends little time with the public.

The throne sits on an elevated platform at the far end of the room. Running up to the throne is a long aisle which shifts into steps nearer the dais. The steps lead steeply up to the large, stone chair. It is surprisingly simple. The seat is bare, uncushioned. The back rest is an oval carved to a point, with the image of a bird in flight chiselled into the stone. Around it are markings, like the loops on the brass doors in the palace. I can imagine Beardsley taking inspiration from this ancient stone chair. I think of him standing here, trying to imagine how he will fulfil the king's latest demand. My heart aches for him. It aches for everyone stuck in this palace with their tyrant king. It aches for the people of Cyne, caught up in the king's quest for eternal life, suffering because he needs money to finance his diamonds; living with the smoke, the bad soil, the dirty water.

After seeing the king's living quarters I know he likes to surround himself in the finest of things. Yet the throne is plain. Perhaps it is the antiquity. Somehow I can't imagine that the king cares about history. His wants and needs are a priority against the history of the realm. No. If he wanted a fine throne, he would have one made. It would be gold and carved into intricate patterns. There would be a fine velvet cushion to sit on and a boy waiting beside him with wine.

The king strikes me as a man who would rather be hunting, or brooding around the castle in his finery, than doing his duties. Tough decisions he leaves to his subordinates. That cowardice sums up the king to me. He wants the title and the glory but not the work. I try to imagine him as immortal. In one hundred years, who will he be bullying then? Will the realm even exist?

I think of the men who have sat on this same throne. Aldrych, Ethelbert, Gregor… men who have been mad or power hungry or weak. Aegunlund has had a bad run of kings. There have been many wars, many years of poverty, too.

As I make my way up the aisle towards the throne I also imagine the many men, women and children who have implored those kings to help them. I wonder how many went away with their problems solved. Few, if any.

With my body tired from the fight, it is an arduous trip up the stone steps. My muscles ache. I move slowly, delaying my ascent to that most coveted of seats. But the suspension only helps to whet my curiosity further. Why am I here? I have been through all the visions now. Is this still the king's fear? What is going to happen? I imagine a riot of people filing in through the large open doors to the room, incensed by anger and searching for someone to punish. I tremble at the thought of being ripped apart by a mob.

It's only when I move closer that I see what sits on the stone chair. It is a crown. I have never seen the crown that the king wears, I have only heard it described as golden, spiked and encrusted with colourful jewels. This one is nothing like that at all. The metal is black and twisted, reaching up like branches. The stones are back, onyx or... black diamonds perhaps. When I reach out to touch the crown, the king appears before me, relaxing on his thrown, one leg thrown out with a mocking grin on his face. I take a step back and a breath escapes my lips, shocked at the sight of his face once more.

Quick as a flash, the sight of the king disappears and in his place is Lyndon. Stone cold eyes stare at me from beneath the crown. His lips curl back to reveal sharp teeth, I shake my head, shaking the sight of him out of my mind.

And now it is Cas's turn, only it is not the Cas I know. He is older, taller, filled out, with a golden beard. His silver eyes are unsure, searching the room. There are worry lines between his eyebrows. He looks as a king should, heavy with the responsibility of his calling. I let out a sigh of relief.

But then the face changes again and I stagger back in shock, my hand coming up to my mouth.

"No, for all the Gods, no," I mumble.

Sitting on that cold, stone chair, is myself. I am still a girl, still awkward with skinny limbs and curly hair stuck out at every angle. I couldn't look less like a queen if I tried. The crown is too big for me. It slips down to just above my ears. My eyes are wide with shock as though I am unaware of what is going on around me, unprepared to wear the crown.

"No," I whisper.

I screw my eyes shut and back away. My back foot trips on the steps, collapsing beneath me. In one uncoordinated move I am falling down, down, down.

My body goes limp as I hit the last step. The room spins, and flashes of images from the visions float around me. The Nix taunts me with more visions of Cas.

"No," I say. "You must stop this. It is time for it all to end." And then I close my eyes.

When I open them, Sasha kneels beside me, singing again, a high pitched melodic verse about a poor farmer's girl who is kidnapped by a nobleman and forced into marriage. My head aches, and my body feels bruised. I lie there and close my eyes. I say nothing, I simply let her continue her song, watching her back, and the way her bright red hair ripples down her shoulders. Marriage. It seems to be what has driven my life so far. I ran from it. I hid my powers. It seems insignificant now.

"You're awake," Sasha says. "I wasn't sure if you were going to come back."

"Did it work?" I ask. "Did I break the curse?"

"I don't know," she says. "I guess it's hard to tell from us being in this part of the castle."

I climb to my feet, groaning at the stiffness in my muscles.

"Are you all right?" Sasha asks.

I bite down on my lip and nod my head, holding back the bubbling emotions beneath the surface. Working through the fears drained me emotionally and physically. It was as though I was on trial and forced to overcome the worst of humanity. The sight of the King's fearful eyes will haunt me forever, real or not real.

"Come on," I say. "Let's explore the rest of the castle."

I pull the lever and the wall drags away to reveal the crypt. I limp over the broken pieces of Beardsley's brass dogs, making our way back up to the basement of the castle. I need an outside door to test.

As we are part way through the basement, Sasha stops. "Something is wrong." She holds up one hand and I watch her body begin to fade away. "It must be time for me to go."

"Why?" I say.

"I don't know," she replies. "I guess my body wants my soul back." She shrugs.

"How can I ever thank you?" I say.

"There's no need. I must be your protector now," she says with a wide grin. "I've never had a job before."

"You've done pretty well so far," I remark.

Her eyes flash with pride.

"Sasha... tell Allerton that I'm sorry... for what I said. There are more important things to worry about now. I think it's time to let go of the resentment I've been harbouring."

She nods. "Of course I will, although if you ask me old baldy needed taking down a peg or two. He is awfully arrogant. Go on now, Mae. Go and wake the others from their slumber and be glad that you have defeated the Nix at its own game."

"Do you really think I have?"

Sasha's body fades further and further until I can see right through her.

"I know it," she says.

"Until next time," I say.

"Until next time."

Sasha fades into vapour, leaving me alone in one of the grand corridors of the castle. I shake my head in wonder. Who knew that ghosts could exist without dying first? I wonder what other surprises there are in the world.

I make my way up to the grand hall, to where I know the large doors open out into the garden. For some reason I am drawn to the fresh air. I long for it. Now is my chance to find out if I really have managed to break the curse. I take in a deep breath, wishing for things to go back to normal. When I have composed myself, I press my palms to the door. In a blissful, beautiful moment, they open, swinging wide and free. My heart soars as I gulp in air no longer tainted with the decaying edge of the Red Palace. Now I can hurry back to Cas and the others, wake them and tell them how I have saved them, how I went into their visions and defeated their nightmares. I'll be their heroine.

But for now I take in the sight in front of me: the long stretching lawns, the extravagant pond, the tall fountain and the colourful floral borders. I hardly notice the weeds poking through the chrysanthemums, or the way the hedges are a little overgrown, I'm too enthralled by the sight of the sun and the green grass; the labyrinth of bushes at the end of the lawn.

Intrigued by the maze garden, I step up onto the little patio overlooking the water feature. Below me, the intricate square patterns are a fluid dance of interlocking green. I let out a small laugh, ready to hop down and return to the castle. But then a sound makes my muscles clench and the hairs stand up on my arms. The smile fades from my lips as I hear the sound of the beast I had hoped to be rid of.

Click-ick-ick.

My heart sinks. The fears were not enough.

The words float into my mind. *That's right, craft-born. You're not rid of me yet.*

I turn, with the strength of wind at my fingertips, but the Nix shoots its paralysing serum towards me. I dive back, twisting my body out of the way whilst tripping at the same time. I cry out as I tumble into the pond, my arms flapping and floundering. There's a scratching and clicking noise as the Nix scuttles forward, and I find myself scrabbling back away from it.

You failed, craft-born. I wanted you for one reason only, to get me the Ember Stone, but you failed.

"No," I shout. "You failed. You were wrong. The king hasn't found the diamond at all. You manipulated me into coming here for no reason. The Ember Stone doesn't even exist," I lie.

Which means I don't need you at all anymore. I don't need this castle, or the people in it. It's all worthless to me.

"You're disgusting," I spit. "You think you're powerful, but you're just an overgrown cockroach with a brain. You think you can rule the kingdom, but you never could. No one could take *you* seriously."

An angry jet of serum bursts towards me and I roll from its path just in time. In an instant I'm on my feet, feeling stronger than ever, and the power of air explodes from me like a hurricane, knocking the Nix backwards. I laugh as it tumbles away from me. Why was I ever scared of this creature? I have beaten its false visions, and now I will beat its body, too.

But the Nix is faster than I'd anticipated. The blast of air knocks it over for only an instant. Whilst I regain my strength, it is scuttling towards me, its teeth gnashing.

I scramble out of the pond and take to my feet as fast as I can, running towards the labyrinth.

You are not half as strong as you think, it says to me.

I hate that voice. I hate the smooth tone, the cold indifference. I hate that it is ingrained in my mind now. It will haunt my nightmares. For the rest of my life.

You should have taken my offer. You would have been very happy with the prince, but not anymore.

"Shut up!" As the anger builds in my body, a jet of flames burst forth from my hands.

The Nix lets out a horrifying squeal, akin to a pig being slaughtered, but it dodges my flames. Now I have no choice but to run. However, I am stuck between the maze garden and the Nix. The space is too open to fight here. There's nowhere to take cover from the paralysing serum. I have to enter the labyrinth.

CHAPTER TWENTY

THE PARTING GIFT

I crouch down between the tall hedges, listening to my own breathing. I'm too loud. I must take control. The air is still and quiet, laced with a tension that precedes a storm. My best attack would be to surprise the Nix. But it is me who is surprised by all this. I had thought that my task was over. How wrong I was.

However there is hope. Allerton was right, the Nix is afraid of fire. For the first time since it began its torment, I have managed to frighten it. I have heard it wail in pain at my own hand. Fire is a power that I have and it does not. I need to make the most of it.

Click-ick-ick-ick.

When I hear that sound it is as though a thousand ants crawl beneath my skin. With the Nix on my trail and the sweet scent of grass in the air, for a moment I am transported back to the Waerg Woods. I'm the frightened girl grieving for her father. But I am not that girl anymore. I am strong enough to fight through the Nix's fear visions. That means I can defeat it in battle as well. I just need to believe.

You cannot hide from me, craft-born.

Droplets of sweat form on my forehead and upper lip as I attempt to form another fireball in the palm of my hand. I inwardly swear as my most unpredictable power fails to come to me. If I cannot do this, the fight is over before it begins. I must believe. I must dig deep within myself.

Click-icker-icker.

The Nix moves closer as my powers weaken. What I need now is time to recuperate, to gather my thoughts and prepare myself to create fire. That's the one thing I don't have. But I can run deeper into the maze.

In an instant I am on my feet and twisting through the labyrinth. The great green walls loom down at me, closing in on me. My chest tightens with panic, but I lift my shoulders and ignore it. I've come too far to let the Nix defeat me at the last hurdle.

Perhaps I can give myself time by tiring the Nix. Even after everything that has happened, I am much faster than it. My body is made for running where as it is encumbered by its own size. I can force it to chase me through the maze. Then I can double back and strike, killing it once and for all. The only problem is: I don't know the maze well enough to be able to do that. Cas showed me around when we first came to the palace, but I certainly didn't memorise the lay out.

When more fearsome clicks sound out, I rush forwards, no longer caring which direction I head. I trip on my heels and take a sharp left turn. It was a mistake. I've come to a dead end. My heart hammers against my ribs as the clicking sound comes even closer.

No, this can't be the end.

I grasp hold of the prickly, thin branches of the hedge, pulling myself up in an impossible climb. My feet manage to find some purchase as I ram them into the centre of the hedge, breaking many of the smaller branches but managing to lift myself higher. There's a splat sound as serum hits the hedge. I'm a finger away from the top, moving just faster than the Nix can spray me with its poison. Sweat runs into my eyes but I can't close them. I just let my eyes burn as I pull myself over the last bit. The Nix sprays its serum at the same time, catching my left foot as I disappear over the hedge and drop to the grass below.

You cannot escape, craft-born, the Nix taunts.

The effort of climbing has left me shaken, cut, and bruised, not to mention the paralysis spreading from my foot. It begins with a tingling sensation, followed by numbness. I have to keep moving before the creature finds me. With shaking hands, I push myself up, but my foot is useless. Almost in tears, I fall to the ground.

Why don't you stop this? It taunts. *I can help you.*

I cry out in pain as more images flash through my mind. Images of Cas. This time, he is indifferent to me, angry even. As I walk the castle corridors he passes me without a second glance. He remains cold and distant, his eyes narrowed.

You were the one who lied to him, craft-born, and he will never forgive you. Look what I can give you.

I begin to move, dragging myself through

the maze. All the time, the Nix taunts me from afar.

Now I am holding hands with Cas. I feel his warmth, his skin, slightly rough, not too soft, not too calloused. He smiles at me. We kiss, and I feel his lips against mine...

"No. This is not real. You cannot force someone to love me, you don't have the power. You want me to live in one of your visions forever so you can control me like a pet. That would be great for you, wouldn't it? You have no real power yourself, harnessing the powers of the craft-born is perfect for you." I shake my head. "I won't fall—"

The next image silences me.

"Father," I whisper.

He is waiting for me at the hut, leaning on his cane, with firewood tucked under the other arm. A crooked smile on his face, humour in his eyes, his mouth opening to talk to me once more.

I try to shake the image from my mind. "No. It's not real."

It feels real.

The maze fades. I'm smaller, lighter, swifter as I run through our garden. My craft sprinkles over our plants, bringing butterflies and Glowbugs to the flowers. Bees buzz around my head, dancing in the air. Father is in front of me and I have only a few strides to make before I can throw my arms around him…

"No," I whisper, dragging my mind out of the vision. "I can't. I'll never come back."

You don't need to, craft-born. Get me the Ember Stone, it's not too late. I know you can. I know it exists. I can read your mind, too, silly peasant girl. Did you forget that?

I have to believe I can do this.

I grit my teeth and drag myself along the grass. Pulling myself forward with my hands and pushing myself with my good foot. There's no way I can give up now. If I can just find a good corner to hide and wait for the Nix. If I can develop a fireball ready to attack it with… I just need… A little further… No, ignore the paralysis. I must believe.

Green hedges everywhere: tall and imposing. At least then I had Cas in the Waerg Woods. Even when he wasn't with me he was looking for me, looking out for me. No one will come now. It's just me and the Nix.

But I am still me.

Click-ick-icker-rick.

I turn to see a jet of serum flying towards me. It comes at me so fast that it propels me up off my feet and with little warning I am thrown back against the wall of leaves. The serum traps me like a fly in a spider's web. Tiny branches poke and scratch the nape of my neck.

I told you I would find you, it says.

"This is not over," I say, struggling against my transparent cage. The paralysis works fast through my body, seeping into my skin.

I beg to differ.

The Nix scuttles towards me, its long, insect-like legs moving in unison, and its shell of a body clicking along. Its teeth clash, gnashing and drooling with saliva.

"Does it hurt?" I ask.

The Nix falters. It stops in its tracks and lifts the neck of its ugly head, the green-black eyes reflecting my own image in them. *What are you talking about, craft-born?*

"The deaths of your ancestors. Does it hurt to think of them? Does the memory keep you awake at night? I know everything. I know how you still feel what they feel—"

Silence.

Another jet of serum coats my face, blocking my airways. For an instant all is hopeless. But I don't let myself linger on that instant. It could consume me, take me whole, but I won't let it. I dismiss that thought as easily as one swats away a fly. I am rage. I am anger. I am fighting against my death and the death of everyone I love. I am heat spreading from my belly. I am fire.

The Nix rushes forward, but I am faster. The ball of flames shoots from me and explodes into the Nix, knocking it over onto its back. It screeches in pain and waggles its legs uselessly into the air.

I struggle against the hard case of the serum. My feet dangle a few feet from the floor, and my arms are trapped against my sides. I can't breathe. It suffocates me, pulling me under as though I am drowning. But I am determined that I can escape through sheer force of will. If I can bend nature to my will, surely I can do this. I can hear the blood rushing in my ear; feel my pulse pounding in my front teeth. White spots dart in front of my eyes. Yet I will not give up. I push and shove. I wiggle and wiggle, rejecting the paralysis in my body, summoning the craft to help me. Somehow, bit by bit, the serum cracks, until it lets me free and I gulp in air.

The Nix shrieks as its flesh burns. The smell is acrid and turns my stomach. My fireball rages on, devouring my foe. I did it. I killed, and it feels... not victorious or powerful... it feels miserable, but also… a relief.

I stand, transfixed by the sight of the flames, but repulsed by the sickening sight. I wonder whether it would be apt to say a few words as this creature dies before me, but what is there to say? That the world will be better without it? That sounds a lot like being triumphant in the demise of a life, and somehow I don't feel like being triumphant. I don't think the loss of a life is something to be celebrated, not even when it is a life so ruined by hatred as the Nix.

Instead of letting hatred overcome me, I wobble forward into the flames and press my hand on its burning body. The flames do not hurt me because I am their creator.

"Take him, wind," I say.

I'm not ready to go yet.

I let out a scream as the Nix contorts its body and clamps its teeth down onto my wrist. A crunching sound rips through the crackle of the flames. The terrible realisation, the sound, the pain, the sight of those black teeth through the flames, it happens in a moment and yet time seems to slow down. It is as though that one second is frozen as I am aware that I'm losing my hand and I can do nothing about it. The crunch was my own *bone*.

My screech sounds into the empty sky as the

blood gushes from a stump. I stagger back, appalled at the loss of my hand, my eyes wide with utter terror.

I hope you enjoy my parting gift, the Nix says.

I hardly hear. I'm too transfixed by my own injury, too appalled to move.

A huge plume of black smoke gathers above the large body of the Nix. My knees buckle beneath me and loss of blood drains the thoughts from my mind. A cloud of dizziness fogs my brain. Tendrils of black drift up into the sky like fingers. They stretch and stretch until they circle the Red Palace. Then they disappear.

My knees buckle beneath me as I fall to the ground. The flames have stopped burning. The Nix is a burnt out husk. I have killed it. At last.

But at what cost?

I wake to the sound of chanting in a low, monotonous voice. A holy man's voice. I haven't heard the sermon of a holy man since I was in Halts-Walden, and that deep tone takes me back to the church lessons. *Celine God of Wind. Take us with your flight, Celine. Holy God of Wind. Protect our village. Keep us from harm.* I would bow my head and think of flying. I was a bird soaring over the land, watching as the fields went by.

There is a grinding noise that breaks the vision of the peaceful Halts-Walden church. It's an almighty sound, topped off with the great clanking of enormous gears. I want to cover my ears, but there is a throbbing in my hand that stops me.

It's then that I realise that I am face down on the cold flagstones of a floor. The church in Halts-Walden rested atop smooth wooden floorboards made from the trees in the surrounding woods. But of course, not the Waerg Woods. They would never build a temple from the cursed forest.

"It worked! Ellen, you are so powerful."

I know that name. It conjures an image in my mind of a beautiful girl. I pity her but am jealous of her. When I turn my head, I see the ankles of the court members. No one seems to notice me on the floor. My right hand keeps on throbbing.

I open my mouth to ask for help when little more than a croak escapes. Around me, the room fills with enthusiastic voices.

"The craft-born is back!"

"We have magic in the Red Palace once

more!"

Ellen's voice says, "Well, I only, I mean… it wasn't anything special."

"Yes it was. It was amazing."

It comes flooding back to me. Everything. First, I remember that my father is dead, and the grief is a tidal wave that would have knocked me from my feet had I not already been on the floor. Then I remember the curse. The sleeping bodies. *I left them in Beardsley's office. Why are they here?*

I must have gone back in time to the moment when Ellen ignited the craft within the Red Palace using my blood. No, I think. This isn't fair. I helped them all and none of them will know. It has all been erased, all the hard work I put in. The fight with the Nix…

Nausea rises from the pit of my stomach. The teeth on my arm. No, no… no! The throbbing in my hand. I can't bear to look at my right arm. What if I really have lost my hand? What if… no, I can't think. I let out a pathetic whimper.

The crowd begins to shift, and a woman in a wide skirt steps on my forearm. The pain is a sharp stab of excruciating pain. I let out a strangled cry and the woman gasps. She stumbles and loses her balance, falling on top of me with a heavy thud. The pain shoots up and down my arm, worse than anything I have ever felt before. It's too much to bear. Dots drift before my eyes and I begin to lose consciousness. There is shuffling, the weight disappears, and I see boots rushing towards me.

"Mae? What...? For the love of the Gods, your hand. Someone call a healer!"

When I wake, the lights are bright and my head is spinning.

"How did I get here?" I mumble.

There is the rustle of clothing and the scrape of a moving chair.

"Mae, I'm here. I'm so glad you're awake." It's Cas's voice. His silver eyes come into view, large and full of worry.

"What happened?" I ask.

"We don't know. After the ritual we found you collapsed on the floor of the castle. It seems you cut your hand on the way down." He pauses, and his eyes drift from mine.

"What is it?" I ask.

"I'm afraid I have some bad news. There was an infection in the cut which threatened to spread. The healer had to remove your hand. I'm sorry, Mae, I really am."

"My hand? But…" Then it comes to me and my stomach lurches. "The Nix, it was the Nix."

"No, Mae, you are confused. You're not in the Waerg Woods anymore. It was just a cut. It was horrible luck, Mae, I'm so sorry. But I'll be here for you. I'll help you, whatever you need. Day or night. I swear… I will." His voice is choked, full of emotion. Raw.

I understand what he is saying, but deep down I know it was the Nix. I remember it burning to death on the ground. I reached out and touched it, said the last prayer… it bit me.

"You should rest."

I stare down at the stump of my hand and the enormity of what has happened hits me hard in the chest. My right hand. My strongest hand.

I may not be a trained swordsman or an archer, but I need my hand. Will I ever be able to climb a tree, or ride Anta, or fight those who wish me harm? I hate to rely on my craft skills. I want to be competent without them as well as with them. I want to be more than a weak girl with some magical powers. Now it is as though some of my independence has been wrenched from me, especially after everything

I did to achieve it.

"I'm a cripple," I say.

"No, you're not. I'm going to make sure you get the best care. You can cope without one hand. You're strong," Cas says. His eyes are bright and glassy. Dewy.

"Strong of heart, stomach, and mind." I laugh. "Maybe I can grow a new one."

Cas frowns. "This has been a shock for you. A deep shock. I think you are a little delirious."

"Maybe," I reply.

Cas sits with me as the healer comes to see me to tell me the grave consequences of the infection in my hand: how he had been unable to save it, but had tried everything. According to him, he has never seen such an aggressive infection and would have presumed that it was a poison if he didn't know any better. Of course, I know the truth. I knew that I could be hurt in the visions. The Nix must have rigged it that way to try and stop me from breaking the curse. Of course, I decided to try and break the curse anyway, and it took my hand as punishment.

The only comfort I take from all this is the knowledge that my injury to the Nix was real, too. It was real enough to break the curse, so surely it was real enough to kill the Nix once and for all. I just wish I had physical proof. Perhaps if its body is still in the palace somehow. No, it can't be. Cas would have told me.

The visions seem insignificant now, yet they were all-encompassing when I fought them. Cas will never know our touching moment in the tunnels, clinging together, desperate and in love. The queen does not know that I solved her problem with Lyndon. Ellen doesn't know how I discovered her secret and helped her face up to her father. None of them know what I did for them, and they never will.

The voice of the healer drones on. Cas's sympathetic touches and words of encouragement are little more than background, all I can feel, all I can taste, is the bitter disappointment that I am once again the one person who loses.

That resentment bubbles up until I laugh. It's a giggle that I can't control, and not the kind of giggle that is infectious and makes other people feel good. The healer gives me a sympathetic smile. Cas flashes me an expression laced with sadness. I can't stop laughing.

"I   have   one   hand," I   say.

Chapter Twenty-One

The Destiny

In the afternoon, the queen comes to visit me. Her eyes fill with tears when she sees the extent of my injuries, but she is as beautiful as ever, her blonde hair rippling to her waist. She wears it down, even though most of the ladies in court seem to wear theirs in braids wound elaborately around their heads. It gives her an aura of simplicity.

"Casimir and Ellen's wedding is coming up soon," she tells me, after composing herself. "I hope you are better by then."

I force a smile. With everything else going on, I had forgotten about the wedding. "Yes, I hope so too," I lie.

The queen examines me closely, as though attempting to suss out my true feelings.

"You know, my son sat with you when you were unconscious. He hardly shifted from your side. He missed meals, he missed his teachings. The king was furious with him, and usually Casimir dares not defy his father."

"He is a good friend," I say with a gulp.

The queen takes my only hand and squeezes it. "Mae, is there anything you want to tell me? About Casimir? Or Ellen, perhaps?"

I shake my head but do not speak, worrying that my voice will betray me.

She lets out a sigh. "I cannot help you unless you confide in me."

"There is something," I admit.

"What is it?"

I glance in both directions, checking we are alone. "I think the king is preparing for a war with the Haedalands."

"What makes you say that?"

"I… I can't say. Only that I have come across information as I've been exploring the castle."

"Mae, you could get yourself killed snooping around like that."

"I'm sorry, Your Majesty, I never meant to—"

She flicks her wrist. "Do not apologise, only

tell me everything you know."

I tell her that I overheard the King's plans regarding the Ember Stone and how he has a secret laboratory. I have to invent explanations for the discovery of these facts, overhearing conversations with Beardsley is one way. The truth is too bizarre, and I worry she will not believe me if I begin to talk about the Nix and the fear visions.

The queen pales as I tell her the story. She worries the sleeve of her dress and stares at a spot above me on the wall. Her brow furrows as she lets everything sink in.

"This is terrible news. You must not speak a word of this to anyone, especially not Cas. He can't know of this. He is already vulnerable as the heir apparent." She shakes her head. "My husband is consumed by power. If he does want to live forever, there is no need for an heir. Oh, this is awful. Thank you for coming to me. I must rally my supporters. I must think of getting my family out of Cyne."

"Can you find enough support to take the throne?"

She chews on her lip thoughtfully. The queen's beauty is only slightly marred by lines around her eyes, lines that suggest experience and troubles. She has lived within the Red

Palace for years, the centre of all kinds of political games. I hope she is wise enough to play the game well. I hope for all our sakes.

"There are dukes in Cyne, as well as some rich nobility in the Haedalands." Her focus comes back to me. "But you are just a child, Mae. You have delivered the news to me, and now you must concentrate all your efforts on healing. Fear not, I will find a solution."

"You must stop him from finding the Ember Stone. I believe it exists, but I don't believe it can be created from the palace. Once he realises, he will go looking for it, and you cannot let him find it, or we're all doomed."

She strokes my cheek. "I know."

My shoulders feel lighter when Cas visits after his mother. He smuggles scones and a pot of cream from the kitchen. We sit dunking the scones and licking the cream from our fingers. After his assurances that Anta is safe and well in the palace stables, and that no, I don't need to get out of bed and visit him, Cas tells me bad jokes to cheer me up.

"At least Beardsley has a spring in his step," Cas says. "The craft magic has the palace singing and dancing again." He bursts out laughing at my expression. "Not literally, Mae. Honestly!"

I blush. "I didn't really think — "

"Of course not," Cas says, laden with sarcasm.

"Are you looking forward to your wedding?" I ask. "How are the preparations going?"

His expression darkens and he stares down at his hands. "It goes well. I have a fitting for my jacket tomorrow. It's very ornate. It belonged to my Grandfather when he was a boy."

The word "boy" hits me hard. Sometimes I forget how young we are to be facing marriage and death. Back in Halts-Walden most people married between the ages of nineteen and twenty-five. If you hadn't taken a spouse by the time you were twenty-five you were considered strange.

"The palace is very busy. Father has guests to entertain for a change. Even the city is bustling, or so they tell me, I have hardly set foot out of the castle recently." His voice has changed in tone from when he told me silly jokes. It remains low, monotonous. Tired.

"You don't sound excited any more. What has changed?"

"I don't know," he says. "I suppose the reality is setting in."

"And what about Ellen? Do you know her yet? I mean, are you becoming… friends?"

"Yes," he says. "We talk."

"And?"

"Well, it turns out that we don't have all that much to talk about. Actually, most of the time we end up talking about you."

"You do?"

"Yes, I suppose you're more interesting. Well, I mean, you're always getting yourself in trouble."

"Yes, that is true." I drop my scone into the cream pot while attempting to use my left hand. "Damn, I suppose it will take time to become accustomed to… this."

"Soon your left hand will be as strong as your right was."

"I hope so. Otherwise it's going to take me a long time to eat, and I don't like cold food."

We both burst into laughter and it feels good to be with my best friend again.

"Tell me more about Ellen," I say.

"She's bright, and can be quite funny."

"But?"

He avoids my eyes and dunks his scone. "Nothing. There is no but. Ellen is a great girl. She's beautiful and a good person." His expression clouds and I feel as though I have probed too far.

We change the subject shortly after that, but I am left with the feeling that Cas is holding something back concerning his forthcoming nuptials. It's natural to be nervous, I would be too, even if it was someone I really loved. But there is something more. What I'm not sure is whether it is my own wishful thinking that sees this change, or whether it is truly there.

That night, Avery comes to me in my dreams.

She is as ethereal as before. Her body is as dark as night and fluid as milk. She wears her nakedness with such complete comfort that it puts me at ease. I've only ever seen myself naked, and not fully. I've seen glimpses in the tiny shard of glass we used in the hut at Halts-Walden. I once took it to the river with me out of curiosity. What I saw was surprising, and for some reason it made me feel shameful. Avery does not make me feel like that.

She feels maternal and beautiful, like the mother I never had. Femininity seeps from her in the same way it does from Ellen. I'm almost jealous, because part of me has always wanted to exude the kind of "girliness" that turns a boy's head, but I could never be jealous of Avery.

"You said that I would lose things in this life. I never imagined that it would include my hand."

Her expression is neutral and I appreciate the lack of pity.

"It isn't over yet, Mae Waylander. This world will throw even more at you. At times I am afraid of whether you will be able to cope, but the strength is there, beneath the surface." She places a hand on my chest.

"Is all this for a reason?" I ask.

"Oh yes," she says. "But it is not written, and it is not definite. I see many aspects of your destiny, but it very much depends on your own choices. Whatever the outcome, I know you will be surprised."

"I don't like surprises."

She smiles. "Does anyone?"

"Am I being controlled by Gods? Because if so, you can tell them to leave me alone."

She shakes her head. "No, not Gods, Ancestors. Your Ancestors are watching and they are here for you if you need them."

"The Aelfen?" I ask.

"Yes," she replies.

Tears spring from my eyes. "What do they

want from me? Why are they doing this to me?"

"I can't tell you, little one. Only know that your strength will help you persevere, even when you are tested."

"How many times am I going to be tested?"

She lets out a laugh that is both beautiful and sad at the same time. "More times than I can count. Some will affect you more than others. All those times will help you become the person you need to be, if you are willing to let it."

I mull over her words. They don't make sense. Perhaps because I have endured too many false images during my torture from the Nix, I now struggle to understand what is real and what is fake.

"Are you another vision?"

"No," she replies. "I'm real. But it is easier for me to come in your dreams. I am no longer alive, craft-born. But my soul lives on, and my soul is here to help you."

"Am I going to die?" I ask.

She sits on the bed next to me. "One day, yes. We all die."

I can't help feeling that she has avoided my question. "Why do I need to be someone else? What's wrong with what I am now?"

Avery leans forward and strokes my face. "There is nothing wrong with you at all, Mae. Not at all. You're just not ready, that's all. And the woman you become. Oh my, she is quite amazing."

"It's all so confusing. I wish there was a clear path for me to walk. I wish there was a sign to follow or… or something."

"This world is full of complexities, little craft-born. The only thing you can control is yourself. In the chaos around you, you are the constant. Believe in you."

She pats me on the pocket of my nightgown. Her smile is warm and friendly, and edged with a little twinkle in her eye as though she knows something I do not. And after she pats me on the chest, she is gone.

I touch the pocket of my nightgown and feel a lump. When I reach inside, I find the king's journal tucked away in there. It seems like a strange thing to give to me, but I replace it and decide that it must be of some great importance. But it is too dangerous to read the journal in this place. Anyone could walk in at any moment.

I lean back against my pillow and try to clear my mind. I'm not sure I will ever be the same again after what I have been through with the Nix. The beast showed me the worst horrors imaginable in those visions, from the crippling fear of death, to the gruesome child murder, to large mechanic killing creatures. Yet, I have a suspicion that I am going to learn there is even worse in the world.

Destiny. It is, by definition, inescapable. I can either embrace it, or run from it. The Mae of Halts-Walden, the one who never washed her face or wore a dress, the girl with the childish sense of humour and mischievous side, she would run away. She has already tried to run away from her craft-born powers. But this new Mae, grieving, brave, strong, and damaged, but with a new view of the world and what she can achieve. She wants to stand up and fight, even if she is physically weaker than she has ever been before.

I should be consumed with anger for what has happened to me. Yet, somehow it has faded. Mastering fire has brought me some peace, made me realise that I can control my anger, and my thirst for revenge.

I look down at the stump where my hand should be. "I am the constant," I say. "I will survive. I will become stronger. I will reach my destiny."

A Note from the Author

A huge thank you for your support by buying this book.

It would be fantastic if you could leave a review on the site you bought the book. I loved writing this book, and love hearing what you thought.

Best,
Sarah Dalton
http://sarahdaltonbooks.com/
https://www.facebook.com/sarahdaltonbooks

ABOUT THE AUTHOR

Sarah grew up in the middle of nowhere in the countryside of Derbyshire and as a result has an over-active imagination. She has been an avid reader for most of her life, taking inspiration from the stories she read as a child, and the novels she devoured as an adult.

Sarah mainly writes speculative fiction for a Young Adult audience and has had pieces of short fiction published in the Medulla Literary Review, Apex Magazine, PANK magazine and the British Fantasy Society publication Dark Horizons. Her short story 'Vampires Wear Chanel' is featured in the Wyvern Publication Fangtales available from Amazon.

www.sarahdaltonbooks.com

Printed in Great Britain
by Amazon

22690657R00189